I refused to believe I was the problem...

DENIAL

de'Jawn Bruner

#BeeInspired Publishing

OKLAHOMA CITY, OKLAHOMA

Publisher's Note: This is a work of fiction. Names, characters, places, and incidents are a product of the author's imagination. Locales and public names are sometimes used for atmospheric purposes. Any resemblance to actual people, living or dead, or to busi-nesses, companies, events, institutions, or locales is completely coincidental.

DENIAL/ de'Jawn Bruner -- 1st ed.
ISBN 978-1-948752-41-1

I would like to thank you Jesus for seeing me through and aligning the people in my life that you chose to get the project done!

It always seems impossible until it is done.

—NELSON MANDELA

Introduction

Now that I have reached peace in my life, I am able to reflect on my past. I was inspired to write this book after reading a blog about living your truth. The author gave me the courage to face my addictions, flaws, setbacks and to basically look in the mirror and own my mistakes. According to Dictionary.com, denial means disbelief in the existence of reality of a thing.

For years, I made myself believe that my relationships and marriage were normal. I felt that all the problems I was having could be overcome with prayer, understanding and hard work. I never had a blueprint of what relationships were supposed to look like because my mother stayed single and the women in my immediate family were not married or even in relationships. I would stay in relationships that were not healthy just for stability. I finally realized by admitting the truth that the marriage I was in was based on lies and infidelity and the relationships I was in were unhealthy.

Who was I trying to fool, them, myself, my circle of acquaintances' or social media? I found out that being in denial was my safe place and I could keep living my life and tricking my mind to think that this is just what my life was supposed to be.

These were excuses I used to believe:

- He loves me the only way he knows how
- He loves me because he light-weight makes sure that I do not want for anything
- He loves me and that is the reason he works so hard and is never here
- He loves me and that is the reason he chose me out of all the women he was dealing with

Why did I even accept that my boyfriend was married or that my husband was screwing around with multiple women at one time, my self-esteem was thrown in the garbage, When did I begin not loving myself ?I lost myself somewhere in between the age of 15-17. It is never too late for change; it is all about learning to accept what you cannot change. The only person I have the power to change is myself. Being in denial is like living a lie and pretending it is the truth, after doing it so long I did not even know the difference between truth and lies. I am powerless and a sick woman, but I will overcome.

CONTENTS

CHAPTER ONE

BORN LIKE THIS

Most children dream of the day they become an adult or obsess about being older, can't wait to drive a car and eat whatever they want when they want. I reminisce about the Toys R' Us commercial; "I do not wanna grow up, I am a Toys R' Us kid" or the character Peter Pan who wanted to play all day and would not grow up, the chorus of the song Forever Young released by Rod Stewart in the 80's rings in my head.

My childhood was lit, I was not a kid that could not wait to become an adult because I was running shit straight out of the womb, excuse my French. Mommy was twenty-six years old when she gave birth to me. She was in love with a married man and lived in Dallas. Mommy said as an infant she was forced to give me everything I wanted, or I would hold my breath until I turned blue. My pediatrician told her that she better give me everything I wanted until I grew out of it or I was going to kill myself. I am not sure that I completely grew out of it. Could I have been born suicidal?

Some people consider high school or college their glory years, my childhood was mine. No doubt I was the biggest tomboy on my block, scarred up legs and French braids. Mommy said she felt like I was in her womb playing football; I can believe it since football is the best sport in the world. The only girly activities I played was jumping rope, hopscotch, and jacks in which my older sister Chris, short for Chrishelle used to tear my ass up and never let me win.

Chris was my rock; she was six years older and took particularly good care of me. Chris used to tell me that before I was born, she saw me in the moon. Chris said she would look up in the moon and see a woman cradling a baby and lo and behold my mom was pregnant with me. Ever since I can remember Chris had tits, real big tits at that. Chris was overly mature for her age and had to grow up quicker than most kids because she had to be responsible for me.

She ran my bath water, combed my hair, fixed my plates and made sure I was ready for school every day, I was basically her child while she was a child. Chris never got in trouble because she was just a pure good kid. I grew up believing she was perfect, and, in my eyes, she still is. Chris has always been responsible, loving and cleaned up without being asked. I was the exact opposite, irresponsible, hateful and did not want to do any household chores. Could I have been born selfish and lazy?

My early years consists of getting up early on Saturday mornings, eating Lucky Charms and watching cartoons. I would ride my bike all around the neighborhood making friends. Momma did not mind my sister and me staying outside after dark if we stayed in the front yard or next door at my auntie's house. I spent rainy days playing Atari and watching Punky Brewster.

We used to pick berries and after my granny checked them, we would wash them and sprinkle sugar on them for a snack. I was just like the boys on my block, I loved jumping fences and stealing fruit out of the neighbor's backyards. I enjoyed go cart riding and skating. I never got a bad grade and momma believed in keeping us busy. I took gymnastic, skating and swimming lessons, I was in brownies until I was old enough for girl scouts.

My family went to church every Wednesday night, and on Sunday's my granny would have Sunday dinner waiting on us when we got home. We would rest a couple of hours and go back to church on Sunday night. We prayed as a family, but I was still a fast-little pigtailed girl who never thought boys were yucky, hell I had two boy-friends in kindergarten. Matter of fact I used to touch and let little boys touch me in the back seat while carpooling in the elementary.

Mommy said that as a baby I loved men, I would smile and giggle when they came around me and would throw my arms up for them to pick me up but not with women. My family used to get a kick out of that when I was baby but not when I got older and nothing has changed. It is hard to admit but my infatuation with men had to have started straight out of the womb; could I have been born heterosexual and flirtatious?

I was the child that never got spankings, I stole money out of the near-est purse whenever I heard the chimes of the ice cream man coming down the block. I used to lift all type of things from the kids at school and was good at it. If I wanted it, I wanted it and if I had to take it consider it lost. This behavior did not stop until it was either me being free or being locked up, hence the reason I have a felony on my record as an adult from stealing from a department store.

I was that kid that rang neighbor's doorbell asking for candy. I was so rotten that if I did not like what we were having for dinner they would cook me something different. You are probably thinking what the hell right? It's true, I had it all but that is because I lived with my two grandma's, not only did I live with my grandma and great grandma but my grandma's sister and her kids lived right next door. Pure bliss, you could not tell me shit, I was spoiled by all and hated by all but it was not my fault, what was mine was mine and what was theirs was mine too, Could I have been born a thief?

My sister and I lived with my grandmothers and two uncles in Okla-homa City. My mother lived in Dallas, Texas. We lived separately because my mom worked over night and nobody liked the fact that we were left with a babysitter all night.

My sister and I were triple spoiled, we both went to private schools until sophomore year, mom used to work two jobs and send money, so we did not want for a thing. My mom was recently divorced from my sisters' dad and head over heels in love with my dad, she stayed in Dallas working and awaiting the reconciliation of their relationship, I am quite sure they were broken up because of his whore-like ways.

I was the youngest of 10 kids that my dad had at the time and remained the youngest for 13 years, to this day my brothers still consider my dad the biggest player of his time at times I feel like I got it honest. I was considered a love child, I was conceived while my dad was still married, they gave me the middle name Love, my dad's name is John and my name means of Johns love, I was born from a full fledge cheater.

My life changed when I was nine years old, mommy moved back to Oklahoma City. She rented a house on the Northside and started working for state. She made my sister and I move in with her. I was sick and was not comfortable with her. I was a baby when I moved in with my grandma's. My sister lived with mommy before and was old enough to remember but I was too young to remember living with her in Dallas, my grandmother's house was the only house that I considered home.

I considered my grandmother my momma, I called her momma and my mother I called mommy. It was a struggle with mommy, I loved her a lot but I felt as if I was getting ripped away from everything I've ever known, it was so painful that I swore I would never put my own children through that, no matter how I struggled, my kids would never live with anybody but me. This was my first time ever feeling hurt and abandonment in my young life.

My glory years were over. I was so angry at momma for allowing mommy to take us, I used to sleep right under her in her California King Size bed leaving the whole other half empty. No more waking up at the crack of dawn drinking our coffee on the porch and listening to the birds sing. I was devastated and an angry child arose. My mom was just trying to do the right thing by taking her kids back but I gave her hell but not because it was in me to do it but because I never warmed up to her, I did not know her.

I was miserable living on an entirely different side of town, momma had a 1700 sq. ft. four-bedroom home and we moved to an 841 sq. ft. two-bedroom home. The house was rented, small and did not have that warm feeling I was used to. I was used to getting home from school and seeing my granny in the kitchen, Uncle Jimmy watching TV in the living room, grabbing a snack going outside to play and waiting on momma to get home from work.

At the new house, I came home to an empty, quiet house where I had no friends. Mommy picked me up from my school's aftercare and Chris would already be in the car. We would get home and either mommy would just go in to cook or she would change her clothes so she could go walk the neighborhood. Mommy used to go grocery shopping once a month because she only got paid once a month and never really bought snack food because we could not afford it. We no longer had the huge surplus of food and snacks that we were used too, so I had to thug it out until the weekends when I got to go back to momma's house. Every Sunday night I would cry going back home, thank God for Chris being there because I hated that dark house called home.

I remember the day I was talking to my first childhood boyfriend, Edwin, on the phone and mommy snuck her nosey ass on the other phone to listen. We were talking long distance, he lived in Talihina, Oklahoma so making that phone call cost his parents a lot of money. We were talking about sex and what we were going to do when he came back to the city. I can hardly remember the content of our nine-year-old sexual conversation, but I am sure mommy knew she had her hands full with me. I was grounded from the phone forever and Edwin ran the phone bill up so high he was never able to call back.

My mother questioned why I was not more like my sister and it used to bother me. I do not know why I was so fast, boy crazy and hated to take baths. I would not have been so bad if she would have just left me where I was. I will never forget the day mommy referred to me as her punishment one Saturday morning in the washroom. It was probably because I did not want to fold clothes and had an attitude. Could I have been born to be my mother's punishment?

My family went to church three times a week, I was happy that part of my life did not change since mommy and momma went to the same church, Olivet. Olivet was a predominately white church and it was only a few black people that attended but I had been going since I was about three years old, so I knew no difference. My granny on the other hand went to First A.M.E right on the same block of our house and the entire congregation was black. I can still hear my granny singing some of her favorite hymns in the back of my mind.

My grandmothers were prayer warriors. Momma and granny always made sure I had Christian books and cassette tapes to listen too. My bedtime ritual was listening to Psalty the Singing Songbook Kid's Praise cassette tapes. I listened so much that I started writing my own songs about God. I was listening to a cassette tape that was teaching about Esther one night and was touched by the Holy Spirit, Jesus touched me; I felt him and immediately started crying and worshipping the Lord. Jesus had touched me in my dark place at a dark time in my 9-year-old young life. I went to mommy's room to wake her up but she was not sleep, I told her I was ready to accept Jesus as my Lord and Savior, mommy prayed with me and I asked Jesus into my heart. This was the best memory I had in that so-called dark house.

Whenever you gave your life to Christ under the leadership of Pastor Crawford at Olivet the next step was to meet with him and discuss Baptism. Since I was younger, he wanted to make sure I understood exactly what was going on and that this was solely my decision. Pastor Crawford baptized me the following Sunday. By this time I had seen plenty of Baptisms, Pastor would come out in a white robe and quote Matthew 3:1-2; In those days came John the Baptist, preaching in the wilderness of Judaea and then he would reach out his hand to the left, the person entering the tub would come from the right down the stairs and into the water wearing a white robe similar to the robe the pastor was wearing. The ritual was to cross your hands over your chest before he leaned you back into the water, he would then dunce your head under the water.

It was finally my turn, It was my day and Pastor Crawford baptized me in the name of the Father, Son and Holy Ghost he ended it saying,

"And Jesus, when he was baptized, went up straightway out of the water: and, lo, the heavens were opened unto him, and he saw the Spirit of God descending like a dove, and lighting upon him this is my beloved son in whom I am well pleased". I remember it like yesterday, and nobody can take that feeling away from me.

I AM SAVED.

CHAPTER TWO

THE AWKWARD YEARS

I was in denial thinking I was grown and knew what love was at ten years old.

Dusk was settling in, it was a very hot afternoon in August, every now and then the wind blew just enough to dry the sweat forming on the tip of my nose, I was ten years old and "in love" with a boy who visited our church with his best friend.

We were at Falls Creek Baptist Conference Center in Davis, Oklahoma a youth camp in the Arbuckle Mountains. Our church owned a cabin along with many other churches, with more than 50,000 young people attending every summer. Attending church camp for those five days was magical without parents and was absolutely the highlight of my summer.

This year was different because I thought I was grown. You see I had my first real boyfriend Monty and we planned to kiss in the woods. Now Edwin was also my boyfriend, since I was seven years old but I was grown now so I knew what I was doing.

Edwin lived three hours away in Talihina and it was considered long distance. I only saw him in the summers when he visited his Aunt. She lived up the street from my grandma's house but this summer he did not come because we ran his phone bill up over a thousand dollars when he left the summer before.

I met Monty at Vacation Bible School. I did not pay any attention to the White boy that was eye balling me and did not realize he existed until everyone was racing to see who was the fastest. Challenge accepted, I took my shoes off and beat their ass. That turned the White boy on, so he told his best friend Aaron to tell me he liked me. My eyes immediately opened up and I realized he was fine, he slicked the sides of his hair back with gel, wore Guess Jeans and basketball sneakers. He was my first White boyfriend but I was not his first Black girlfriend. I was told he only liked me because his other Black girlfriend moved out of state and I reminded him of her because I was Black. Monty was experienced with girls because he used to watch his older brother. Solange, my friend at church, told me I had to close my eyes, tilt my head and keep my lips slightly open so he could slip me the tongue, I was terrified.

We made it to camp, and I do not know if I was sweating from how scared I was or the heat but I was light headed and about to pass out. We planned to kiss on our way to worship service that started every evening at 6:30 pm. The walk from our cabin to the worship center felt far but this evening it felt closer than it had ever been, I was nervous. Monty took my hand and I followed him into the woods, it was the sloppiest and most awkward first kiss. But we got better and started kissing every chance we got, I was in love.

Just like in any relationship, if you never see the person or talk to the person there isn't a relationship. Summer was over and Monty never came back to our church so technically we broke up. I was still crazy about him at thirteen and still stalked him by calling and hanging up in his mom's face. I managed to always meet people who went to his school, so I attended his school dances just to look at him. I was in DENIAL that he still liked me; this is where my stalker path began.

Mommy had me isolated at Princeton, a private Episcopal college prep school that was all white kids. My choices of having a boyfriend were slim and I was done with White boys. I hated mommy chose that school because I was tested and put back a grade. I was mad and embarrassed to do the fifth grade twice. I made straight A's on my report card before, but mommy said Princeton was well advanced and it was important for college.

I hated my home life and now I hated my school life. I went to school with kids that made me realize we were not rich. I did not fit in and a few of the teachers Mrs. Vick and Mrs. Ream looked down on me making me feel like I did not belong there. I was embarrassed that we lived in the neighborhood across from the school and did not want to be seen walking home because all the other kids lived in big beautiful homes. I wanted to make friends with kids I could relate too and not feel ashamed about what we did not have.

My life revolved around church because we were there every day the doors were opened. Cheryl was my best friend at church, she was a caramel skinned beautiful girl with bleached hair. If there were a chance I could go to her house, I jumped on the opportunity. Cheryl was popular and a comedian, she had a lot of friends. Cheryl went to public school, I thought she was so lucky. She got to wear whatever she wanted. I had to wear uniforms. She got to eat nachos and pizza for lunch, we had formal sit down lunches.

Cheryl had a persuasive personality and even though we were the same age she was a role model. She said we were never going to have sex and stay virgins, so I stuck to that for a while because I did not want to let her down. I met most of my Black friends through Cheryl and she had my back, she was very protective of me because she knew I had not seen much. She hooked me up with her boyfriend's friends or cousins. I got sick of double dating at the dollar movie with the not so handsome best friend or cousin.

We were virgins, we called ourselves V's and proud of it. We made up our own clique, my name was Pimp Dawg Day Love, my middle name is Love so it was perfect. Cheryl's nickname was PDQ it stood for Pimp dawg Queena because Cheryl's full name was Queena LaCheryl. We had another friend, Sonnie, we called her Short Dawg because she was 4'11. We had so much fun being "pimps". Pimps in our mind were just players who in our case just played and talked to multiple guys but none of them could get none. At this time, we were not even sixteen and driving so we would get dropped off at Crossroads mall or go to school games to have fun.

I had a boyfriend at church, Corey he was full blooded Indian. I had known him for over 6 years but really was not interested until we were freshmen. Corey was sweet and quiet but on the basketball court a whole different person, he had swag. That boy would ride his bike almost four miles to my house every day after school while my mom was working a second job. He kept money in my pocket and the first boy who saw me naked. Every day after school, I had field hockey practice when I got home, I would immediately jump in the shower. I would leave the front door unlocked for him. One day he came straight in the bathroom and saw my naked silhouette in the shower. I knew what I was doing. Another day he ended up one day just jumping in the shower with me. I never looked down once and we never had sex. Our relationship was cool but that did not stop me from talking to other dudes because I called myself a player and I had to live up to my name.

On the eighth day of March my life changed drastically, it was Cheryl's birthday and she got her car. This meant we were free; we were at all the events looking good and going to see all our boyfriends. I would see everyone except Corey because he was still fifteen and I needed an older boy with a car. I broke his heart. Cheryl met David a guy from Spencer, I could not wait to see the new guy I would get hooked up with. I hooked up with Stu's neighbor J-Love. J-Love just like Day Love, I was excited. J-Love was an eighteen-year-old senior with a slope haircut, he was a part of a dance group and he was so sexy and to my fifteen-year-old tender freshmen ass, I was in heaven.

Now that Cheryl had a car, I did not have to wait until Friday to get away, she would pick me up during the week and we would go out to Spencer. J-Love lived with his stepdad and had a lot of freedom. Cheryl dropped me off at his house and would go up the street to David's house and then picked me up on the way home. We would not do anything but dance, we called it freaking and J-Love was good at it. I would just sit in a chair and he would dance on me.

Everything was going good with J-Love but after three months of seeing each other we had the conversation over the phone about having sex. What was I thinking messing with an eighteen-year-old thinking he was not eventually going to bring up sex? I told him next time I saw him we could do it, but I really did not want to have sex with him because kissing and dancing was all the steam I needed.

The time had come, it was a Friday evening in May, I remember J-Love was about to graduate, he had his cap and gown on the bed. He asked me was I ready and I replied, "ready for what," playing dumb because I knew exactly what he was talking about. I was not ready but after asking me twice my lie and reply was yes. J-Love turned on his Guy slow jam cassette tape and grabbed a towel. I asked him what the towel was for and he said because I was going to bleed. I said what you mean I am going to bleed? I grabbed my shoes without putting them on and ran up the street to Kiki's house.

I called J-Love from Kiki's phone and told him I am sorry I freaked. I explained that I was not ready, and he told me that it was okay. He told me he loved me, but I did not believe him because he started showing me less attention. So now when we went out to Spencer, I was usually chilling by myself because he was not home, without breaking up, we just fell off, I was not upset at all.

Summertime in Oklahoma City was hot and boring if you had no friends that lived close. At fifteen years old, I did not want to go outside until 7pm or I would get musty. I begged and pleaded with my mom to send me to Douglas High School with Cheryl but her answer was no. Then one day, I politely fixed my lips to say I would flunk out of Princeton. I basically told her the thousands of dollars in tuition would be flushed down the toilet, so she quickly changed her mind. Okay de'Jawn you may go to public school, but it won't be Douglass, you can go to Northeast. I felt like damn this woman would do anything to keep me from my best friend but if she knew what she knows now she would have let me go to Douglas, my entire family went to Northeast so I guess it would still be cool, Northeast it is.

My mom was very strict, I was probably the only fifteen-year-old that could not talk on the telephone after 10pm. Cheryl and I had a code, she would call and let the phone ring once and hang up then I knew to call her back. Cheryl had her own phone line and answering machine, so she could talk all night if she wanted too. I returned her call and she said guess who just called me asking about you, I got excited "Who girl?" I asked anxiously. "Denzel, girl he asked me to ask you to call him, do you still know his number?" "Nah, tell him to call me now," I replied. I used to call time and temperature when I knew someone was about to call. So the call waiting would beep in my ear instead of ringing to wake my mom because she would have answered and embarrassed me.

Denzel called and I answered nonchalantly because the last time I spoke to him he had broken up with me. We had not had a long relationship but long enough for me to know he was someone that could spice up my life. Denzel went to Putnam City West and lived with one of his aunts because he had some behavioral issues at home. Denzel and his cousin Israel came by my house a few times on the weekend when I dated him during the past school year. I remembered the butterflies and goosebumps on my arms when he took my hand to pull me close to kiss. I remembered thinking he had soft lips. I asked how he had been and told him the way he broke up, I thought I would never hear from him again. Denzel was a smart ass, he replied oh really, well you thought wrong, that broke the ice and we both laughed.

One night while on the phone with Denzel, I told him I was driving to come see him. I did not have a driver's license and was not sixteen, but it did not matter to me because I could drive. I learned when my mom used to take walks in the evening, I would sneak her car to teach myself how to drive. I had never taken drivers education classes, but I felt stable behind the wheel. I told him if I was not there in twenty minutes to call an ambulance. Denzel said he was going to be outside waiting and praying. My mother went to bed pretty early at night and the keys were always on the dining room table, so I had easy access. Her car was not parked in the garage so it was really easy for me to sneak out of the kitchen door that leads to the garage and out the back door because she always kept her bedroom door shut.

It was about 11:30 pm when I pulled out of the driveway. I was nervous but I wanted to see him so bad. I put my seat belt on and made sure my headlights were on. I stayed inside the lanes and never swerved; my mom had a tiny Toyota so it was easy for me to maneuver. I pulled up around 11:45pm, I felt like a pro. Again, here come the butterflies and goosebumps.

As I sat on the hood of my mom's car, he stood between my legs to get as close as possible. His hands on my waist, I felt the warm tip of his tongue slide across my upper lip as I opened my mouth slightly to let him slip me the tongue. He smelled like Johnson's baby lotion and I was all the way taken in. We talked outside until about 4am, he kissed me and I headed home thinking he smelled so good. Once I got home I snuck back in the house, quietly put the keys back on the table, tiptoed to my room which was right next to hers and called Denzel to tell him I made it home, then like we always did, we stayed on the phone until about 6am.

This went on for the rest of the summer. I took her car every night. Tyesha was friend since we were four years old in pre-school at Capitol Day. She was my partner in crime and she definitely was not a virgin. Her boyfriend was a drug dealer that was at least ten years older than her. He kept her pockets fat, bought her school clothes and to fifteen-year-old girls this was a big deal. Tyesha and I finally got caught stealing the car but it was not my mommy's car it was my sister's car. We did not want to take Chris' car, but she should not have parked behind mommy and by this time I was so addicted to sneaking out that it did not matter whose car it was. When Tyesha and I got back home around 5am all the lights were on in the house, we were like daaaaaaaaaaaaaaaaaaaaaaaaammmmnnn!!!!!!!!!!!!

We acted like that was the first time we ever did it and we were sorry. We lied and said Tyesha left something at her house and we had to go get it. Stealing the car continued for me, my mom started parking her car in the garage. I was so good that I would flush the toilet and raise the garage at the same time to block the loud noise.

Recap– I was in denial about my behavior. I was a child of God and running in the wrong direction. I was boy crazy. I wish my mom would not have been so strict then I may not have been so fast. Denzel was not a good influence on me, he was in a gang. I liked his bad boy image, we were not cut from the same cloth. We were brought up totally different and had different beliefs. Corey was a better fit. I wish my mom would have been okay with me hanging with Cheryl, I believe my life would have gone down a different path.

CHAPTER THREE

BULLIED

WHOLE NEW WORLD, *I was in denial thinking that I would fit in with no problems at a new school, when I was sheltered my entire life.*

What the hell did I get myself into? I was so out of my comfort zone. My first day going to a public school was unforgettable. I saw my first pregnant teenage girl. I saw Crips and Bloods, this was a whole new world, but it was too late to turn back now, this is what I thought I wanted so I embraced it. At my old school I was a cool chick but at my new school I was called the preppy girl that talked white or the girl that thought she was white. I was excited to see one of my childhood friends, Dedra, but I could tell we were not going to be friends like we used to, her group of friends were nothing like me.

I did not know where I fit because I was not a gangster or a thug or stoner. I was not a band member or a rich girl. Going to school at Northeast felt awkward, I did not want to be in the circle with the preps or with the kids that you can tell parents had a little money because that would be too much like what I just left. It was too late to be in a fall sport because I would have had to be enrolled in the district the spring before to make the team. I was definitely a mix between a jock/prep, but I had no outlet to find people like me to hang around.

Denzel and I were still going strong seeing each other almost every night because I still stole my mom's car and drove out to Bethany. He would come home on the weekend which was around the corner from

Northeast. He came to pick me up in his brother's jeep one Friday after school and that is when I had a new identifier at school - Denzel's girlfriend. Denzel was popular which made me known at this point because before going to PC West he went to Northeast, so he already knew everybody at that school and had a lot of fans.

School was still just school. I had AP classes, so I was surrounded by smart kids and still looking for a way to make some friend. My classes were full of seniors that I really did not have anything in common with. I really wish I was not in any of those classes it was hard enough to find people to connect with. I heard on the school announcements and they had fall cheerleading tryouts for basketball coming up. I had been a cheerleader since I was in the 7th grade so I knew I would make the team.

Cheerleading try outs were the same day fall break started. It started off great, I smashed my tryout and was cleared by my grandmother to spend the day at Denzel's house. Denzel and I watched television. We play fought on his waterbed and during all that he managed to get my shirt off and bra with one hand. I grabbed my shirt and ran holding my A cup size breast in my hands all around the house while he chased behind me trying to see. I was so embarrassed. I was not ready for him to see me like that yet plus I had a keloid from the chicken pox on my right breast that was a conversation piece.

His older brother, Tommy, came home from work and let us take his truck to the store. On the way there we saw a girl from my school, Kara. She got very mad seeing us together, I was confused. Denzel told me it was nothing to worry about and that she just liked him a lot. He told me he saw her earlier that week in passing and she cried because she saw my picture on the pendant of his necklace. That was extreme and felt like something to worry about, but he reassured me it was nothing.

We watched television and talked, it had been a good day nothing was on my mind but going home and calling him like I normally did but Denzel had something else in mind. We went back to his room and laid on the waterbed listened to music and kissed. Kissing led to him taking my clothes off and I did not know what to do. I knew I was not ready but I thought I loved him. He talked me through it. As he put himself in me and it was the worst pain I had ever felt in my life. I wondered why people liked it because I did not. I had some bleeding and shed a few tears; it was not worth it. Denzel and I did not have sex for a second time for about three months.

School had become abusive. I was fitting in the cheerleader world but was getting bullied by Kara and her crew. I had done nothing to them. They did not like me because of who my boyfriend was, threatening to fight me, looking at me crazy while I walked down the hall. I could not understand why they gave me hell over a dude, it was so hard to get up and go to school. I prayed every day that they would leave me alone. I hated myself for choosing to leave my school to come to school where I could not even concentrate on getting my work done. At school I was just waiting on the next crazy thing to happen, a hard head makes a soft ass.

My life at school was rough but my love life was precious. Denzel and I grew closer and closer. He was my best friend and we spent as much time as we possibly could together. It was May and school was almost out for summer break, I had survived the year but my grades had not. I spent as much time away from school as I possibly could, I would need to go to summer school to make up some credits. Not only that but I was feeling like crap it was hard to get up every day and I was having stomach issues. Denzel bought me a pregnancy test and I am a statistic 16 and pregnant. I had only had sex maybe four times and now I am going to have a baby. Denzel was so excited that I was having his baby he treated me like royalty.

I moved into my grandmother's house because my mom was so upset about me getting pregnant. Summer classes started the middle of June and Denzel took a class as well that he needed to make up. He picked me up every morning from my grandmother's house in his blue Delta with no AC. I thought summer school would be fun because this would be the first time Denzel and I went to school together. His mom agreed that he could move back home and transfer back to Northeast. The upcoming year would be Denzel's senior year and my junior year in which I was not looking forward to because I was enrolling at Emerson, a school for pregnant girls.

The first day of summer school should have been my last. The first people I saw were Kara and her crew, I thought to myself why God? I could not catch a break, seems like I was being punished for falling for Denzel. I was in love with this guy, he was so nice to me and I knew he would do anything for me. He treated me with respect and protected me to no end. Of course, the girls were giving me hell and one day after school Kara's crew acted like they wanted to fight me.

So, Denzel was about to fight all them, he was so angry pushing them out of the way and calling them all bitches. Why was I such a target, why did they all take their aggression out on me? I had no clue, were they trying to punk me into leaving the love of my life alone?

I hated summer school. Denzel told me, those ghetto ass bitches are jealous of you and want to be you. But for the life of me, I could not understand why? I had done nothing but be cordial to these girls, it was not in me to be anything else. I was not a hateful person; my heart was pure with no mean streaks. The problem was I feared them, and they knew it, they knew I did not want any problems. I was nobody's fighter. I wanted to be friends with everybody. As summer school continued, the more I was picked on the more Denzel showed me love because I would be so upset, and questioning should I be with him. Denzel bought me dinner every single night whatever I wanted to my grandma's house and that made me feel special. I never questioned where he got the money because he damn sure did not have a job. I knew he was selling drugs.

I went to Emerson the following semester which was my junior year as planned. Denzel was around Kara every day now doing Lord knows what. I had my baby December 6 by C-section the hardest but most precious moments ever in life. I had so much support, my grandmother watched him every day when I went back to school in January. Denzel moved into my grandma's house and I do not think I could have been happier. Parenting was fun and Denzel was a great dad. He would get up in the middle of the nights with our son and let me sleep most of the time. I would hear the occasional rumor about Denzel and Kara from time to time, but he assured me that NOTHING was going on and I believed him.

Denzel went to college the following year. Langston University about 45 minutes away from the city and came home on weekends. I do not know if I had gotten pregnant in the summertime or on one of those weekends, but I was and not keeping it. It was my senior year and I was not trying to have two children. We got our money together and went to the facility to have an abortion. I never really thought about it much until it started bothering me a few years later. Life was good I had a car, a part-time job, school was not that bad except for when I ran into Kara and her crew.

Four months before graduation and I am pregnant again. Could things get any worse? Kara and her friends were giving me the blues. The morning sickness was awful. My life felt unbearable, but I could not mentally handle another abortion. How did I get pregnant and I am taking the pill? The doctor told me it was because I was inconsistent. Denzel was distant and the relationship was not the same after he found out I had cheated. I figured he should have gotten over it just like I had to get over whatever he was doing. One morning in February I decided I could not handle one more day of torment from Kara, I quit school and got a full-time job.

My life was going nowhere, Denzel treated me like an obligation and not a priority. He was in the streets now selling drugs, cheating on me, and not going to school. I was so hurt; this was not the guy I fell in love with. I was broken. I had recently caught him at a motel room with a freak that was feeding him nothing but lies, she told him that I was messing around with this guy at work but the extent of us messing around was flirting and a kiss on the cheek. I can remember it like it was yesterday, it was a Sunday afternoon it had to of been around 12pm check out time.

I knew he was at the Remington Inn because he and his boys always stayed there, it was cheap and close to the eastside where we lived. I headed up there ready to fight because my gut told me he was there with somebody. I pulled into the parking lot and bingo there was his friends' car. Now either I could sit outside and wait for them to come out or I could go bang on every single door.

As I walked in with a queasy stomach and head hurting, I shed a few tears, this was the first time I had ever stepped foot in this motel/hotel but was walking through like I owned the place. I begin to knock, and Denzel came to the door and I immediately started swinging like a windmill. The girl was just grabbing her stuff while Denzel just kept throwing me on the bed to keep from hitting me. When I finally ran out of the room, I went to the roof and looked over. I wanted to jump but all I could think about was my son. What it would do to my family? Did I really want to go to Hell? The devil taunted me for over half an hour because I stayed up there weighing the cost. I was mortified, pregnant and wanted to end it all.

Why did not I just leave this guy alone? Why did not I love myself more? Why did I feel so lost without him? Would I always take him back? The end of what was supposed to be my senior year was hard because I let those girls get to me. Now everybody was walking across the stage getting their diploma but me. I wished I had listened to my mom and stayed at Princeton, my life was hell and not getting any better. I quit my job and totaled my car on my birthday, and I was 7 months pregnant. The wreck was so bad that Tyesha flew out of the window but walked away only bruised up. My son did not have one scar because he had come out of his car seat.

Pregnant with a child, 19 years old, no car, no job and living with my grandmother. Denzel and I were back together but I was miserable most nights. There was a rumor going around that Kara was pregnant and had slept with Denzel on prom night. I tried to not let it bother me because he just kept telling me that she was a liar and if she was pregnant it was not his, so I believed him.

I had my daughter October 15th, I was in love all over again. Once again, I had a C-section leaving me with a longer healing process. Denzel's grandmother gave him her house because she wanted us to be comfortable. We moved in about two weeks after my daughter was born. Denzel slept every single night with his daughter on his chest. I would have the perfect little family if he was not such a cheater. We had been living in the house about a month and the rumor of Kara being pregnant with Denzel's baby resurfaced. I asked him again and he was so frustrated that he called her. There was no speaker phone so he put the phone between both of our ears and asked her why she was lying about being pregnant by him. He cussed her out and told her to leave us alone and that was not his baby, so again I believed him.

Our first Christmas at the house was just another day, we did not have jobs, but my kids got plenty of presents from our families. The gas was off in the house and we had to boil water to bathe and use the microwave to eat. But this was the least of my worry because I missed my period in December and was pregnant again. One night around 2am, I woke up hurting so bad and passed a blood clot in the toilet. This was embarrassing my daughter was three months old and here we go again.

Denzel left the house on Valentine's Day and never came back. I stayed up waiting for him. I paged him and he never called back. I did not know what was going on. When he finally came in the next day, I was devastated I knew something was wrong. He told me Kara had her baby and that she was his. How was I supposed to process this? He told me the entire time that the baby was not his. At this point I think I should have been on meds because a part of me died that day.

My entire pregnancy with my third child was depressing, there was not one night that I did not cry myself to sleep. I felt hopeless. It felt like every time I went to the doctor; I had a new venereal disease. Then one day, I came home to Denzel and Kara snuggled up on the couch. I just went in our bedroom and cried myself to sleep, I was numb. The thoughts that were running through my mind that night, I could have killed them. Thank God there were no guns in the house. I woke up the next morning to the sound of Kara and her baby leaving. I knew I had to leave but I took my time just trying to process what was going on. Denzel did not love me anymore and for the first time I knew he loved Kara. That night, I packed up the little belongings my children and I had and moved back to my grandmothers.

I would use my sister's car from time to time and go by Denzel's house. One time I went by, I saw some professional baby pictures taken of his daughter and I burnt them up. Another time I went and broke out his window with my fist almost hitting an artery and was rushed to the hospital, I had lost my mind. When I had my third child, Denzel did not show up on time, I cried giving birth. I was so hurt that he did not make it to see my son being born. I was over everything.

Recap– I was in denial, believing I was ready for a family. I was in denial, believing just because a girl knew he was my boyfriend it made him off limits. I was in denial, believing a bully would leave me alone if I ignored them. I was in denial, believing I could forget about God and make my own decisions.

CHAPTER FOUR

SELF-INFLICTED

I was in denial I did not realize I needed professional help.

It is a proven fact that hurt people, hurt people. I am three children in and twenty years old. My life could not be more depressing. I felt I had nothing good going and could not believe that I had done this to myself. Who was this person? What happened to me? I had no ambition, no goals, no get up and go, my only drive was to follow behind Denzel, stalk him and make his life a living hell for doing me like this. It was hard to follow behind him with no car which made me even more depressed. I did not realize just how mentally sick I had become, my whole life revolved around a man that did not love me or my kids. I spent most of my time feeling regret and hating myself for having three kids that I was not emotionally or financially stable to take care of. My grandmother, mother and the state were taking care of them. I did not want children without the father. I wanted the family, if I had known I was going to be a single mother I would not have had any.

Moving into my first low income apartment with my children alone would be problematic. I did not have any help and I realized that child endangerment was real. I was accustomed to having in house babysitters, being alone was not good for me. I was still so immature and needed guidance. If I was not so hot headed, then I may have slowed down and taken the time to realize just how much I needed counseling. I moved into Oakridge Village apartments when my youngest was about two months old. It was winter and the gloomy days did not help with my mood. I felt so lost, alone and stranded because in Oklahoma City the transportation system was sparse and if a bus did run close to your home it shut down at 6pm. I was nowhere near a bus stop and the drive from the street down the driveway into the apartments felt like a mile long. I had no choice but to make friends within the apartments.

First people I met were my neighbors in my building. My apartment was a downstairs backside apartment. Denysee a hairstylist had a front upstairs apartment that was diagonal from me. She lived there with her daughter Megan and had a steady boyfriend that was there often. I started going up there to chill when she was off work if her boyfriend was not over. I met Will and Bill, Will lived next door to Stacey and Bill lived in the next building. They were both 17-year-old and juniors in high school. I met them bringing in my groceries they stopped to help me bring them in. Will and Bill were nice boys, they were not hood or nerds, but they did not seem like they were popular either.

I told them they could come by whenever they got out of school to chill. They were three years younger, but it is not like I had anything going on, so I needed the company because I was always in the house with my kids and no house phone. They took me up on my offer and started coming over every day after school. We all became cool, Will and Bill both had brothers that were two years younger that would occasionally come by and chill.

Life in the apartments was boring, I felt like I was in prison behind those gates in the woods. Denzel would come by to bring pampers and milk every other week and I would be angry every time he left because I wanted him to stay. Most of the time he was in and out but a lot of the time he would have sex with me and leave. I still wanted to be with Denzel, and I was not ready to give up even after all we were going through, it pained me to think that he may be at his other baby mommas house.

I rarely left the apartments, I left on Thanksgiving and Christmas and other then that I was stuck. New Year's came and went, and I had no resolution, I just chilled in the apartment with my kids and my homeboys that came over every day. I was not even thinking about a job, I was severely depressed, and the only upside was getting the knock on the door from my homeboys every day after school, even if it was just listening to what they had going on. Occasionally I would get my friends car while she went to work and go sit at Denzel's house, I was desperate to see him.

I spent day in and day out with my children, I was there physically but not mentally. I had no church life or prayer life all I felt was torment.

My cousin Kiko always filed my kids at tax time so all I wanted to do after getting the money back was get another cheap cash car and stalk Denzel. My stalking consists of going to all his friend's houses beating on the door or to show up at the house on 28th street and causing havoc. It did not matter where he was, I would always find him and no matter what he was doing I would automatically start fighting him even if one of my children were on my hip. I had broken so many windows at this point that all his friends knew when I pulled up it was on and crackin.'

Spring was approaching and I was still settling into the single baby momma life. I had often flirted with Will when the guys came by calling him out on being scared to have sex as if I was so experienced. I knew he was a virgin and I always thought he was sexy. Will was an athlete, he stood 5'8 with a muscular body type. I was attracted to him because he was nothing like Denzel. Will was sheltered, he lived with both parents and was the middle child of seven siblings. He was a good son, passionate about his family and had a good head on his shoulders, he spoke of going to the military after he graduated.

Will and Bill were on Spring Break from school and could stay out late for the week, I told him earlier that day he did not know what he was missing and needed to find out. I was all talk; I did not mean anything I said. In my mind, Will was never going to fall for it so I felt safe being aggressive but this day I got a knock on the door late that evening. I was scared and it was time to back up all I said. I could not send him away and I did not want to hurt his feelings. So as awkward as it was, we went back to my room. I took my babies to their beds and had sex with him. Afterwards he said sex was overrated and I felt the same way. Sex is as much mental as physical. I learned that night if I were not into a person emotionally, sex would be a waste of time. I thought about Denzel the entire time. I told Will we had to have sex more for it to get better and eventually it did.

I started having sex with Will consistently and thought I loved him, it did not matter to me that he was three years younger, he was a breath of fresh air, no drama. Growing up to realize that love doesn't hurt I can say that my feelings towards him were very strong, I always wanted him around and I knew if I was not so torn up behind Denzel we would have had a chance. I missed Denzel but at least I was in another relationship.

My children were not in good hands. Even though Will and I were a thing, I still was an unfit parent. It started off by me leaving my children while they were sleeping and walking to the pay phone inside the apartments. I would be on the phone sometimes 30 minutes to come back to them either still in the play pen or in bed sleep, so I felt like they were not in any danger. I used to run across the hall often leaving my kids, it became a bad habit. I always lived with someone before, so I never had to worry about my kids being alone.

I considered myself in a relationship with Will but still running behind Denzel, we were not having sex, so I did not feel like I was cheating. The only reason the attraction was not as strong as it could be is because he was still in high school and lived with his parents. Besides that, the sex just was not enough to keep my interest. His family hated me and rightfully so because I was not good for Will. I was a nice person with a huge heart, but I just had too much baggage. The older you get the wiser you become, and they had me figured out.

Sherrie was an entertainer, she always had strangers in and out. She had a guy come over her apartment named Lenny, he was a blood, real cute and had a great personality. I chilled for a while and went home because Will was over. I must have sensed there was someone over her house I wanted to meet because later that evening. Will left and my kids were sleep. I went back over and Lenny's cousin, TK, was over there handling some business with him. From first sight I was star struck. TK stood about 6'1 with a slender frame, he was a mixed breed with green eyes, dressed to impress and I was completely mesmerized. He was a blood as well and I had to have him. I had never had a one-night stand but there is a first time for everything. We had an attraction for each other and having sex with him was explosive. This was not like anything I had ever done or would ever do in the years to come. I thought this would be my first one-night stand instead I was trying to be his woman.

I was infatuated with TK, he had my nose wide open and he knew it. I was so intrigued by everything, Denzel sold drugs but he was not doing it like TK. TK only messed with doctors and lawyers other than that he had his little homies working for him. It's not like I had that much game, but I had enough sense to know what I was dealing with. I swear he upgraded my mind. It's like once you've opened Pandora's Box you cannot shut it. I hated myself for doing Will like this, I honestly did not know rather I was coming or going. I was a broken woman that had been played so much that now I guess I am playing the same game. When TK came by the whole world stopped. I did have enough respect for Will to only meet him across the breeze way at Sherrie's house.

TK was in a relationship with a woman that was a lot older then us and I could care less. I was whipped and would take anytime he would give me which was not much but it kept me excited and looking forward to the next encounter. TK was the elder of two brothers, he took care of his little brother DeWayne nick named Killa. I instantly loved his brother, he was around thirteen years old and lived with TK because their mom was in prison. I was still with Will but TK made me feel alive again, he gave me butterflies, he made me nervous being in his presence. I wanted to be into somebody else besides Denzel, TK just did it for me. I used to gather clues like Inspector Gadget trying to figure out where he lived. One day talking on the phone he said I am going to 7-11 to buy blunts. I asked are you going to the 7-11 on Aaront and he said no, on Classen by my house. I drove my raggedy car over there and went up and down all the streets close to Classen looking for his car not caring about my license being suspended. I knew that my car would run hot and stop if I stopped at a light or a stop sign, but I went anyway. Eventually I got pulled over by the police. I gave the police my sister's social security number which at the time was your license number was given a ticket and went on my merry way. Three months later my sister got a letter in the mail stating her license was suspended. She was so angry at me, I said what did you want me to do go to jail and she said no, but you could've told me and paid the ticket. My grandma paid for it because she always bailed me out.

It did not matter what I had going on in my life, some things never change which was my daily hunt to find Denzel and get in his business. As long as I had a car in my possession he was going to deal with me one way or the other. I knew where all his friends lived and somebody would always give up his spot. My play brother Jamie which was Denzel's best friend always had my back. I met Jamie my first year at Northeast and he was a senior. If I needed anything he was there, he bought plenty of pampers and milk, I can honestly say he was truly my kids uncle. He was the only friend that Denzel had that never tried to talk to me. Jamie was moving weight so a lot of the time he just handed money over and did not even mention it to Denzel.

TK was pushing weight as well and hit a lick on a bird of cocaine. This was major weight. He told me he was moving back to Colorado so he, packed their house up and left. It was late November 1996; I was so hurt. I finally had a little spark in my life and now it was gone. I got a house phone so that TK could call and ended up getting it cut-off because his mom called non-stop from prison talking to me about nothing. I was still messing around with Will and he was a senior now, but I knew we had no future because even while with him I was thinking about Denzel.

I met Noel in February 1997, she was 18 years old and seemed to be cool. She was a hairstylist in the apartments giving everybody fGinger waves. I heard her name circulating around a lot. They said she liked to fight, some said she was a whore, others thought she was cool, but everybody said she was on drugs. My first impression was she was a lot of fun and we kicked for weeks. TK's middle brother, Tony, was one of Noel's friends with benefits. I met him at Lenny's house and he instantly started calling me sis, he was in jail when TK and Killa left.

Sherrie knocked on my door to tell me TK was on the phone, he called her apartment because my phone was off. I told him I was going to rent a car to come see him. I had known Noel about four days, she was the perfect person to go because she had no kids, no job and no agenda. She was basically a nomad. I paid this older guy that lived in my apartments to rent the car for us and I took my kids to my grandma's house. Noel and I the road about 10pm and arrived in Colorado about 6am the next morning.

Walking in TK's apartment, I immediately got the bubble guts. I had not seen him in almost three months and had never spent an entire night with him. His apartment was decked out like I knew it would be. He had a huge fish tank with exotic fish, having a nice fish tank in your house was a necessity back then. The apartment was completely furnished with a woman's touch. We hugged. I took a shower and got in the bed; we had driven the entire night; we were all exhausted.

I stayed four days with TK and they were wonderful. We had a good time even though we basically stayed in the bed the entire time. We were not ready to go back to Oklahoma matter of fact we were trying to figure out how we could move there. We stayed about three more days and was broke, we did gas runs all the way back home. Back then you could just pull up to a pump and start pumping gas, gas stations expected you to pay once you finished. I was too embarrassed to tell TK that I did not have any money to get home for fear of him thinking I was irresponsible. I had no game and he should have paid for the trip in the first place and would have if I had of just asked. The rental car we had was three days late so when we got back, we dropped it off at a nearby church and called the rental car business and told them where it was. I was four days late picking up my kids from my grandma's house as well, they were pissed. I was immature and did not care how my choices affected other people.

Will graduated in May and we were cool, I did not tell him anything about TK. His family hated me so much, so we did not spend as much time together. I think they called Child Protective Services (CPS) on me and if they did, they were within their rights. I left my kids at home too much, I thought I knew their sleep schedules well enough to make runs all over the city. I would tell Will's little brother to run in the house and periodically check on them to make sure they were sleep. I had favor with Christ because one day Will and I ran to my sister's house and when we got back a woman was there from CPS. I believe because my kids had a clean home, nice bedroom furniture, a toy room and plenty of food they never created a case. It taught me a well-deserved lesson, I slowed down because as much as I was an unfit parent; my kids gave me a reason to live.

Father's Day 1997 was a turning point in my relationship with Denzel. I had not seen him for a while, and it turned out he was living with Kara. The kids and I went to buy him a Father's Day gift and took it to his job. I could tell he missed us he asked that I come back to his job in a few days. Within a few weeks, he was back living at his house with his dad on 28th street and we were back together. I got a tattoo on my right leg in big letters that said DENZEL GOLDEN #1 it looked terrible, but he was proud of it. The relationship with Denzel this time around was different of course because he knew it was not all about him like it used to be. I was not the same girl that fell in love before plus he had two kids with Kara. I kept my apartment but spent most of my time on 28th street. We had a toxic relationship, but I was addicted to him.

I met Brenda, and Patrice the day they needed a ride to the store and instead of me taking them I just gave them the keys to my car. You see Patrice lived with Brenda because her son, Lonnie, was Patrice's baby daddy. Patrice started coming over a lot spending time at my apartment and we became good friends. She was going through hell with her baby daddy and I was going through hell with mine, so we had that in common. Neither one of us ever smoked weed before and decided to start together, we would get high, paranoid, laugh and eat. We had a great time; I had found true friendship. Patrice and I seemed to be on the same level, we just clicked and became inseparable. Patrice became family, we started taking my kids to their papa's house and going to the club. I felt like I was living again, since my entire life did not revolve around Denzel. I hooked her up with Jamie, I thought he would be perfect for her to get her mind off Lonnie and his shenanigan's. Patrice still lived with Lonnie, but she kept catching him cheating. Lonnie loved Patrice he just made wrong choices, like so many of us. He was not as disrespectful as Denzel was, but he was still scandalous.

Patrice was the reason I defeated my high school bully. Patrice and I went over to the house on 28th one night looking for Denzel and Kara was in his driveway. As usual, Kara was talking reckless, Patrice said you better get out and beat her ass, so I did. Kara never saw it coming, she did not even get a lick in. After that I wondered why I was so scared of her in the first place. From that day forward, I kicked her ass every time I saw her. I would visualize our next run in and meditate on what I would do to her. Out of all our fights I do not think she ever hit me once, I was too quick, shot out to Taebo for teaching me how to fight.

I moved out of Oakridge soon after, I was approved for a house on section 8. I did not move far approximately two miles away. At this time Denzel was hustling hard, I had money stashed away in shoe boxes. Most times he would come bring money and forget he gave me the money for a certain item and give it to me again. I was stacking, I did not pay rent, I had food stamps and the bills were not high. I do not know how much rock they used to sell but it was enough that the feds had my phone tapped and was sitting outside my kid's daycare snapping pictures. Denzel knew he had to get out of the game quick.

Recap– I was in denial because I should have taken parenting classes. I was in denial, believing because I was mentally ill I would be excused from hurting Will. I was in Denial, believing time apart from Denzel would make our relationship better. I was denial, believing I could make it without God.

CHAPTER FIVE

UNSTABLE

I WAS IN DENIAL, I BELIEVED I WAS STRONG ENOUGH TO GIVE MY CHILD UP FOR ADOPTION.

Denzel and I were only back together for about a month and I found out I was pregnant again. Only this time I was not keeping it. You see, I was the queen of finding out late, I was already close to four months along. My life was just at the point that it was getting better, I had gotten my GED and about to enroll in college. I missed the three-month mark to get an abortion, so I called an adoption firm, I was not keeping anymore of Denzel's kids. I had three and that was enough for me. Denzel was pissed, he said I better not give up his child. Denzel kept me stacked with money expecting that I would keep the baby. I bought a Honda Accord and threw some rims on it, gave Patrice the money, and kept saving. Denzel was too unpredictable, and I finally realized I had to take care of me and mine.

My unborn child had a military family from Missouri that would call and check on me periodically, they were a white family and excited about getting their little black child. I was in denial that there was a baby growing in me for fear of getting attached. I wanted the pregnancy different from the last three pregnancies, I went to a different doctor and a different hospital for delivery. This baby was going to be induced that way the adoptive parents knew exactly what day to plan for their bundle of joy.

I went into labor a couple of weeks shy of the due date, I did not call Denzel because he was hurting about my decision and already told me he would not give up his paternity rights and was going to fight the adoption. The only person I had in my corner was my mom, initially when I told her I was pregnant and giving the baby up for adoption, she cried but if that was my choice then she would stand by it. She started to build a relationship with the adoptive parents because she wanted to always receive pictures of the baby and they had an agreement.

My mother met me at the hospital when I went into labor, I was prepped, medicated and mentally ready to have the baby and hand it over, until there were complications. My mother was fine with seeing and holding the baby, but I chose the opposite. I heard my mother scream this baby isn't breathing he's turning blue, I freaked out my baby was dying. They worked on him and determined they needed to medi-flight him to the same hospital I had my other three children. I called Denzel and told him to rush to the hospital to see his son, he was dying and flying him to Baptist Medical Center. Denzel was escorted by the police up to the hospital room, he was in a high speed chase on the highway with them and did not pullover until he got to the hospital, he got out of the car with hands up screaming that his baby was dying and the police helped him to the room.

Denzel was frantic when he came in the hospital room which made the situation worst, I was already in a terrible head space, he told me if I gave his baby up for adoption he would kill me; I lost it. I was screaming from the top of my lungs what do you want from me, I am sick of you, I hate you. The doctors came in asked him to leave and sedated me, I went to sleep. My mom left for Baptist before my baby left and was there minutes after they arrived, she was not leaving her grand babies' side. When I was released from the hospital, I went straight to over to see my little boy. Once I saw how sick he was, I told my mom I could not give my baby up, he is sick.

There was no way I could stomach giving up my child to the parents waiting on me to sign the adoption papers. I was at that hospital every day all day looking after my last child. I got my tubes tied in the hospital right after he was delivered, I did not care how many fines I had to pay and if I had to pay the adoption agency back for the rest of my life. I did not see this coming; he was supposed to be healthy; I was not supposed to see him. He was born the fourth of May and the court date to sign him over was the fifteenth of May. The adoption agency did not sue me and decided not to recoup any monies they spent on me because they knew I was genuinely unstable.

Tommy Denzel Golden named after his oldest uncle did not want for anything, Denzel went on a shopping spree for him. I was happy with my decision; I am four children in and decided to enroll in school. I started at Platt College in August to become a dental assistant, I always wanted to be a dentist since childhood, but my life went in the opposite direction. School was going great and life was looking up, I felt like I was headed in the right direction. I was being a better mother, woman and was handling my business.

My grandmother was Ninety-seven years old and not missing a beat, my best friend in the entire world and had my back like no other. I did not even see my utility bills because they went straight to her house. As old as she was, she still tried watching my kids, with the help of her daughter, momma. granny still cooked every day. I got a call that my granny had fallen in the hallway, it always broke me down when she fell. She would say oh I caught a fall today and I would cry. I am sensitive, I cry if I see an old person walking in the street, I pray when I hear an ambulance. I fussed at her about using that walker, we all did. This fall sent her to the hospital she had broken her hip, I was devastated. I talked to her that night and cried to her telling her to not die on me and she said oh DayDay I will be fine. They told my granny she would have to go to a rehab, and she told us she did not want to go, I knew in my heart she was not coming home. Granny asked to see Tommy and my mom came and got him and took him to the hospital, everybody told me not to come because they did not want me bringing all the kids. I got a call at school the next day to come say goodbye to my granny she had a stroke and they were keeping her on life support until we all got there. I was grateful she got to love on my last baby, I was grateful for everything, my granny is in paradise enjoying her well-deserved mansion. My life would never be the same, I went into depression, it was like I had post-partum six months after Tommy was born. I did not want to do anything, see anybody there was a dark cloud over me, I was not the same.

I smoked weed to eat, I smoked weed to sleep, I smoked weed to study, I rolled over as soon as I woke up in the morning after opening eyes, before my feet hit the floor and smoked weed. I did not care about anything but taking care of my kids and finishing school because my granny was proud that I was finally trying to do something with my life. Denzel still made sure that Tommy had everything.

I started working at Horace's supper club as a waitress on Wednesdays and Friday nights. My aunty Sue got me hired, she was a bartender. I needed a job because Denzel was not coming around as much and stopped selling dope after the feds were watching. Wednesday nights was strictly for men, they had exotic dancers entertaining and I had the entire floor. My pockets were full of tips and numbers, I was not thinking about Denzel. Denzel could not stand me working in the club with all those men, he hated it so bad that he came in the club and asked me to marry him. I was shocked, he hated me in the club that much that he wanted to lock me down. I said yes, we went the next day to the courthouse to get a marriage license and the following day we got married.

Denzel tried doing everything he could to live a legal life, he was frustrated. He was accustomed to bringing in stacks and working a regular job was not him. He had ambition and dreams; he just did not know how to put his plans into play. I watched him struggle trying to start a lawn service, a car washing company and he could have been successful if he would have saved money he was making while hustling.

I completed the program at Platt and was now taking classes at the community college. Married life was great for about eight months but then Denzel got restless. When Denzel did not have any money, he was a miserable person multiplied by ten. I was taking finals and my first semester taking college courses was almost over. It was normal that I came home from school to Denzel on the couch playing video games but this day I came home to silence. I watched television for a while in my bedroom and noticed Denzel's clothes were out of the closet, he left me. I did not see it coming, I was blindsided and distraught.

I was used to him running but I thought this time would be different. Why would this man marry me just to leave me again? I searched the city looking for him but did not find him anywhere. I went and picked up my kids from daycare a blubbering mess I could hardly keep my composure. I could not call him because cell phones were not popular yet, I could page him but if he did not call back there was nothing I could do. I did not show up to take my exams, I was not in my right mind to study, and all I knew to do was cry. He did not call his kids for Christmas; I was done, and I meant it

I started selling crack, I watched Denzel in the kitchen cooking it before and remembered somewhat how he did it. Patrice and I decided we were going to be drug dealers; Juvie gave me some to sell but that did not last long. I was selling it all to Noel until I could not do that anymore because I loved her and hated to see her like that. Noel introduced me to this older man named Roosevelt. He would distribute it for me.

Working at the club was fun, I met a lot of people young and old. I decided to work at Horace's and the Plumtree to stay busy. I worked at Horace's on Wednesday and Sunday and at the Plumtree on Tuesdays and Sundays, making good money. On Sunday nights at the Tree they had open mic and it was entertaining watching the rappers and sGingers, I thought to myself that is what I wanted to do. I could not sing but I felt like I could always rap and wanted to since the fifth grade.

I met Jeff Bennett they called him Juvie he was great on the mic, I watched a lady called Natural Red, she inspired me. I started free styling to the beats on the juke box, one Wednesday night at Horace's two men came in to order a fish dinner. One of them introduced themselves as Priest and asked for my number, he was fine, I gave it to him. He said he was a rapper. Priest called the next day and asked if I could come over, I had my kids and told him it was not possible maybe next time. The next night I worked he came in with another man that he introduced as Yung One, I lost all composure, Priest was fine but Yung One was grown man sexy and gangster. There is no way explaining what I felt at first sight, I just knew, I knew he was the one I would go coo-coo for cocoa puffs over. This man instantly had me feeling some type of way, his smile was everything. I told him I gave my number to Priest, but I wanted him, he said he was digging me too.

Valentine's Day I had to work at The Plum and my homeboy Juvie bought flowers to my job, he was so sweet, I went home that night and Denzel was in my house, he had rose petals in my bathtub and on my bed, I thought to myself what was he doing at my house, I should've changed the locks, I was over him. I had sex with him because it was Valentine's Day, but I felt nothing. My mind was elsewhere, I was thinking about the fine man I met and could not wait to kick it with him.

What was up with me? The last man that had me weak was TK, I fell for TK because I liked the way he handled business, and he was about his bread. Yung One had a mysterious look about himself; he was not the loudest in the crowd, he was laid back. What got me was the way he looked at me, it was like he could see straight through me. The fact that he was a rapper had me intrigued because I wanted to be a rapper. It did not seem like he had much money, Yung One was special, a millionaire in the making. I did not want to be a fling to him, I wanted to be his woman. I was not going to have sex with him until we got to know each other.

Yung One was quick to invite me over to the Turbo house just like Priest, that is where all their groupies were invited. Turbo was a rapper as well; he was my friend Sherika's boyfriend. Turbo was the leader of the group; he handled the major business. He had a house where some of the artist that were a part of his group and signed to a major record label chilled. Turbo had a van that was wrapped with his logo for promotion, everybody called it the Turbo van. I saw Yung One five days straight either he invited me to his studio session or over to the Turbo house. This was until he had to turn himself in for thirty days to the county jail. When he got out of jail we no longer went to Turbo's house, we went to his mom's house. We started having sex from the day he got out. He was very protective and did not give a damn about Denzel. One night after the club was over, Denzel and I were arguing in the parking lot and Yung One pulled up like superman with his crew in the Turbo van, grabbed me out of the confrontation and smashed out, he did not care who I was with or who I was leaving. Turbo was concerned our relationship would cause problems with them being signed to a major label, he told us we had to be careful.

I began working on my album at Diamond Sound Studio, it was Dre Jackson's home studio, and the best in the city. I started off with Zion but Yung One told me I needed to use his producer and engineer Keys and so I worked with both. I met a man name Israel at the studio and after he heard me, he said I would never have to pay for studio time again. He meant it too, he had an investor that later that week wanted to meet me and put the deal in place. We recorded a couple of tracks and Israel wanted to move my kids and me to Atlanta. We were selling CD's out of the trunk for seven dollars all undone tracks, but they were going like hotcakes. I met Jaz and Sneak, Sneak was Juvie's friend and we all did music together and opened for major rappers that year. Israel was teaching me a lot but Yung One did not like him much especially when I told him, Israel set up a meeting with a music attorney in Atlanta to listen to my music. Israel was down for me as down as they come, he treated me like I was the next best up and coming artist. He got my pictures taken and made sure I was in the studio faithfully. As far a marketing went, before I stepped in the club he had the DJ's announce me like I was making a special appearance.

My sister let Israel drive her car to take me to my meeting in Atlanta and my mom kept my children. I had an Astro van that would not have made it three hours away to Texas. We had our meeting and the music attorney was impressed he said what most said, she's a diamond in the rough. He told me he wanted me to move there so he could put me in a better position to make my dreams come true. He worked with big names as the like of Mariah Carey and Baby Face's so for him wanting to take me on as a client was a celebration indeed. I celebrated by having sex with Israel, why God, why did I do that? Sex ruined everything.

Yung One did not want me to move, he felt like if he was back and forth from California working in the studio then I could be back and forth from Atlanta but I did not see it like that. I was excited to start my new life and chase my dreams. Men can always sense when a woman is messing around with someone else because when I got back from Atlanta he was on my bumper. I still wanted to leave the city. My life was different now anyway, my granny was dead, I was not with Denzel and he barely saw the kids. Kendell turned Patrice against me telling her I was looking at him like I wanted to get with him. Noel was still heavy on the drugs, I continued flushing them down the toilet and it did not matter she would start right back up using. I wanted out. Kara and I were not beefing since she knew Denzel was not around anymore. She had the nerve to come by my house and tell me she wanted to record music, I felt like everything I did she wanted to do. I was back in church heavy, so I wanted to make peace with everyone plus I felt like God said it was time to move.

Tommy stayed with my momma for the summer, Missy went to Buffalo, New York with her daddy, ManMan and Dugga stayed with my daddy. Israel and I went to Atlanta, we had two months for him to get a job, get us an apartment and get our feet wet before we went back to get the kids. It did not take long, Israel started working at his sister's beauty shop as a barber in Marietta and we stayed in Mableton with his cousin for a few weeks. I traveled back and forth on the greyhound the entire summer. I paid for everything by selling CD's, I came back to the city to get Noel as soon as we got an apartment in Atlanta.

While Israel was working, Noel and I were downtown selling CD's and getting to know the city. We were invited to So So Def studio's and missed our appointment trying to figure out how the train and Marta worked, Atlanta was a whole new world for us. It did not matter what studio I walked in, they offered me a contract, I would take it back to my attorney and he would turn them down. He did not want me signed to a label that did not have a good reputation.

Summer was over and I came back to the city to get my kids and pack, I put my van in the shop so I could get everything fixed. I packed the house up and gave away everything but our clothes. The van being completely road worthy was holding everything up, it needed everything but a new motor. My kids had to start school in the city until we could leave, Israel was in the city as well cutting hair but still paying the rent in Atlanta. It was September 11th and the United States had just been bombed. We were all in a state of shock I did not know if moving was the right move, it all seemed surreal. The news made it seem like we all needed underground bunkers, I did not want to leave my grandma's side.

Recap- I was in denial believing, I could get away from my problems by leaving the state. I was in denial believing I could make it in the industry without a solid team. I was in denial believing, my friends drug problem would not slow us down.

CHAPTER SIX

BATTLEFIELD

I was in denial, believing everything did not come with a price!

I was in denial believing I was in good hands with Israel, he was just as sick as I was but in a different way. He could handle my sickness but I could not handle his. I was a fool to think I could have a music career, work with other male producers and he was not going to be jealous. We moved to Atlanta with the kids October 1ˢᵗ, we only had two bedrooms, so all my children were in one room. I enrolled them in school and got a job at the restaurant Martin's next door to our apartments and Israel worked at another barber shop down the street as well. This was the first and last time I worked at a fast food restaurant, which was hard work. Working at Martins only lasted a month because I was looking to find a bartender job at the closest club. I started as a waitress at Vegas Nights, I knew how to bartend, thanks to my Aunty Sue but a bartending position was not open. I worked Friday and Saturday nights and started off making about four to five hundred a weekend after a year I was making around six to seven hundred because I had my regulars so by this time I did not want to bartend.

All Israel and I did was fight, I could not keep my hands off him I was sick and that was the only way I knew to communicate when I got frustrated; I would fight. One night I hit him in the head with an iron and my son was screaming for us to leave. ManMan kept saying let's go to a shelter mommy. I could not handle Israel' drinking problem and he could not handle my mouth; I agree it was reckless. We moved to Town Homes when the lease was up about three months after we got there not far from the apartment, they were nice. Israel let his uncle G move in, Greg was an older veteran around 65 years old that did not have any family in Georgia. We needed help with the kids, and he helped by cooking and cleaning. I went to work on Fridays at 4pm to set up because they had a happy hour with free food and live entertainment, it was my best night.

The maintenance man at Oakridge had to come by and fix the garbage disposal, it was my first time meeting him, his name was Teon. He was around fifty years old and he looked at me like a steak. He was not my type but he was real sweet, he let me know if I ever needed anything I did not have to call the office but to call him directly. I thought to myself, that is never going to happen in this lifetime, until he started coming by bringing me lunch. He looked out for me and there was not anything I could not ask him for, it's nice to have people like that when you're so far from home but everything comes with a price.

Israel and I fought every other day, he had a routine work and to the liquor store. The music grind stopped because he wanted and needed to keep a roof over our heads. Israel meant well and he tried, I just could not talk to him because he stayed drunk and emotional and I stayed high and nonchalant. I thought I loved him, but I honestly did not know what love was and never felt love from a man. I have felt passion, I have felt lust, but I did not know love.

Living in Georgia, I was in survival mode, no relaxing because if you do not work you do not eat. I was used to having section eight and food stamps, we did not have food stamps in Georgia for about a year because they said I had to sign papers to put Denzel on child support, they did not do that in Oklahoma.

I made some good friends the first year in Georgia, I went to the American Legion down the street from my house, locals called it the Legion, it was jumping. I met a lady in the bathroom, her name was Ginger she was a beautiful woman with the cutest hourglass shape. The first question she asked was who does your lashes, I told her I did not wear lashes and we laughed. She said she just moved from Detroit and gave me her number; we instantly became friends. My friend was about her paper, she had two teenage boys and they lived about two miles from my place. Marcia lived in Atlanta and I had five friends from Vegas Nights that I hung with, Tarcha, Toya, Summer, Liz and Niecee. We had fun making our money and going out during the week and after the club. Tarcha was the stylist of the group, dressed her butt off. Toya was the bad ass of the group, she had a mouth on her, leave it to Toya to be in the corner talking crazy to a man and they loved it. Summer was the hazel-eyed sweet one of the crew. Liz was the African Princess and knew all the scams and Niecee was the white girl that only dated black men, could out dance plenty black woman. Noel was still around but she was making her own friends, she knew she had an open-door policy at my house, she only came when she was tired of partying for a few days.

Israel said he wanted me to make it in the music industry, but he gave me hell anytime I had a session. I rode to the red train on a Wednesday night to listen to open mic, I worked as a waitress for a couple of months so I knew the staff. Walking up to the door I hit a doobie to get a quick buzz and the security held me in handcuffs until the police arrived and arrested me, put me in a patty wagon and took me to Cobb County Jail. I called Israel and he was there within minutes with a bail bond getting me out. It did not matter if we just had a disagreement, he felt responsible for me and had my back. I stopped smoking weed that day, they put me on probation, drug tested me every month and I had to do DUI school. The day I got off probation, I went to Ginger's house to smoke and that was the last time I touched it. I did not feel like starting over with getting paranoid and having the munchies, weed used to calm now it scared me and made me hungry, I was done.

Teon asked if he could pay me to stay home from work on Friday nights about once a month and he would give me five hundred dollars. It would have to be a night that Israel thought I was at work, I made to much money on Saturdays. Friday I would drive over to the next complex over, park my car and Teon would pick me up and drive right back in our apartments to his place. He cooked for me, we watched movies and had sex. He took me back to car around 1:30 am so I could get home around the time I normally did leaving the club. He became my sugar daddy only he caught feelings and I had none. Every time I left Teon's house he would tell me to leave Israel, it became a struggle.

I met Johnny at Vegas Nights. He came in every Friday night for happy hour, he was a scientist and worked for the Center of Disease Control. He had it going on, he asked me to come over and he would pay me to take a picture topless, I went and he paid me three hundred just so he could put me on his wall of fame. Johnny had about two hundred pictures of naked women on his wall. We never had sex but he became one of my best friends. When a woman told me they were in bad shape, I would hook them up with Johnny. If Johnny thought they were fine, he would pay them to take pictures. That was my boy, he loved me and my kids. He had a big heart and I would not take just any woman around Johnny. If I thought a woman was on drugs or was crazy I would not allow them to kick it with him, Johnny was a doctor and career oriented, I was protective of him.

I was walking out of the grocery store one afternoon and a man stopped me, asked for my number. He said that he wanted to take me shopping. I was gullible, I believed him. His name was Alex, a diplo-mat for Jimmy Carter. I got over to his beautiful house and he did not want to take me shopping he wanted me to put on lGingerie and have sex with him. He dangled four hundred dollars in my face, I was so mad, I left. I saw him at the store three months later and he said I still want to give you the money to go shopping. This time I went by his house and gave him what he wanted and I got what I wanted. He be-came a regular sugar daddy like Teon.

Yung One flew to Georgia, I was excited. He did some work with Ni-tro the first day and stayed with his friend the rest of the time. His friend stayed three minutes away from my apartment. I spent all day with him with no sex. Yes, I did have a few sugar daddies but one thing I was not doing was having sex for free, that was not happening. I had Israel for that, he was shocked I would not have sex with him. He went on and on about how he could not believe Israel had me like that. Israel did have me like that, I was not having sex mentally with my two sugar daddies it was just physical. I made them wear con-doms, I was always tipsy and damn near scrubbed my skin off in the shower afterwards.

Denzel came to Atlanta to see his kids and when I mentioned it to Is-rael he got upset. Denzel stayed from Thursday to Sunday. He picked the kids up and took them to a carnival on Thursday. James, a man that liked me from my job took us to Dave and Busters and paid for everything because I said Denzel was my cousin from out of town. We took the kids and kicked it at Johnny's house on Saturday and on

Sunday before he left I had sex with him. It was not the same at all, there were no feelings involved. I argued with Israel telling him I did not come to Atlanta for love, I came for music. The next day he took off work and took me to Def Jam South to let them listen to some of my music and they hired me on as a writer.

I hooked up with and ran around the city the entire summer, they took me everywhere with them. I think they were trying to figure out my character to see if I was a hoe, I did not have sex with any of them. I hung out with an entire popular rap Family. I just knew I would be their first lady. I spent the summer waiting on beats and to get in the studio what did they have me around for, I needed a manager to nip this in the bud.

My grandmother who I called momma was getting sick. She was retaining so much water that she was placed in the hospital. Since my granny died momma had not been the same, she loved her mother and lived with her almost all her life. Momma did not do anything but sit on the couch after granny passed. Momma was not affectionate, she never said I love you, you just know she did. She called to talk to me and when she got off the phone she said I love you. That was the first time she had ever said that and the next day I gotta call that momma died. I was sick, my uncle's friend paid for Ja'Waun and I too fly back home for her funeral. I hurt so bad remembering how momma was my best friend and how granny had to take her place in my life because I felt abandoned. To cope with momma's death, I pretended that momma was still alive and I was just out of town.

I moved in with Teon, I did not want too but Israel left the apartment and I could not pay the rent. My kids went back to the school they were originally going to Dunlieth Elementary. It was probably the happiest time of Teon's life but I was miserable living with him. We only stayed there two months because Ginger's best friend, April, wanted to move out of her apartment and said I could take over the lease. I was so happy to get out of the house with Teon, that was God. I was working as a bartender across town at a strip club Strokers, but I did not always make great tips. I needed another income and there was a restaurant opening about a mile away from the apartment called Raul's. It was a Puerto Rican restaurant and I was hired on as a bartender.

The staff that was hired at Raul's was awesome, It was new and everyone was eager to learn the menu and learn the signature drinks, while training I met Daniel, he was hired on as the restaurant manager. He looked like Shemar Moore but Puerto Rican with beautiful curly hair. He made it clear that he wanted me out the gate, he came on strong and let it be known. I was talking to some of the younger guys and they were talking about where to get some weed from, he told them I got her she can get anything she wants from me with a serious face, the guys were like dang okay. I was not even asking for weed because I did not smoke anymore.

Our relationship moved quick, he had a house down the block from the restaurant with a roommate and I was still in the apartments. He left his roommate and we moved into a house together within a month. Daniel loved my kids and my kids knew it, there was no way to have my regular guy friends tagging along with this man in my life, he was not going for none of the foolishness. He went into a rage because I did not invite him to the parent-teacher conference at my kids school, he said they were his kids and he wanted to be on all of their paperwork. He was family oriented and he wanted to marry me, when I told him I was married he teared up and told me I needed to handle that ASAP.

My kids told me they needed to talk to me, Raymond said remember a couple of days ago when you said if anybody ever touch us we better tell you, as my daughter hid her face in the pillow, he told me Greg touched Missy. At that moment my life flashed before my eyes, I screamed I am going to find that nigga. I called Daniel while he was at work and told him to come home, I was losing my mind. I felt like I did not protect my child from a monster, I felt like I was the worse mom, I sank into depression. When I told Daniel what happened he cried and told Missy that he was there now and nothing was going to happen to her again.

Daniel wanted his niece Ashley to move in with us, Daniel had one sister and one niece, his parents passed years before. They lived in Philly and soon his sister wanted to transition to Atlanta. Ashley called Daniel uncle Dawg. She was my daughters age beautiful little girl, mixed Puerto Rican and black with long, thick hair that was hard for me to tame. Ashley was well-mannered and loved her uncle Dawg. She started school with my kids and everything was fine for about eight months until Daniel let her mom, Maigin move in. Our relationship took a turn for the worst, it felt like she was the woman of the house. They were close and Daniel finally had family in Atlanta, I get it but I felt like he pushed me away. It used to be us making decisions but now it was them making the decisions. I felt like she was jealous of anything he did for us.

Marcia called and asked if I would waitress Jermaine Dupri's last night of Birthday Bash in Decatur. I waited on Brandy, Jermaine, Nelly, and Iverson and the place was packed. Gunshots rang out about midnight and everybody fled the building besides Nelly who was still walking around turning bottles up. Someone snatched DJ. Clues necklace and the shots rang out. I still had all the money in my apron from the bottles that they ordered and was told we needed to leave. I went home and counted 5,000.00 and moved my family to a house around the corner from where we were.

Sick, Sick, Sick these men made me sick, I made myself sick. Here I am again depressed crying out to God. Why is it that as soon as Daniel was done with me, I looked into getting divorce and got a tattoo of his name with a rose on my breast. As cocky as I was about making money that all stopped because I did not have anybody to watch my kids while I bartended at night, I started looking for a day job. James Holmes owned his own collection agency and he hired through a temp agency, I was hired on for 10.00/hr but I needed 15.00/hr to pay my bills. Ginger and Nakia worked there too, it did not feel like a job. I began an affair with James, he was married with no children, we had sex all over his building. The court made me take anger management classes for beating up Daniel and his girlfriend so I had to take off during office hours and James still made sure I was paid for 40/hrs a week. It did not matter if I only worked 15 hours, he would sign off for 40 hours. James was at my house all evening and I saw him all day, he kept saying he was leaving his wife.

Marcia's daughter Jace, we called her banana girl was my heart. My kids and I loved that baby so much we would beg Marcia to let her spend the night. James's Friday night hang out was Applebee's so I packed up Missy and Nanaboo and headed to the restaurant. The waiter walked us to our table and Nannaboo saw James and screamed James. He could not help but smile but his wife looked at him like she wanted to murder him and me.

His wife was not to be played with and she made my life a living hell. One night, James was leaving my house and she was waiting for him outside. Another day, she followed me to church and told my pastor I was messing with her husband. She ordered my birth certificate. She called DHS and told them I was selling food stamps. But James still left her, he moved his clothes in and was back at the house getting more when she called the police on him. She lied about him beating her up. James spent six months in jail for making terroristic threats.

Niecee moved in too help pay rent, the basement of my house was just as big as the upstairs, minus a kitchen. She had three kids but only the baby boy stayed with her at the time, he was two years old. She was chosen to go on Flavor of Love so I agreed to watch him. Flav gave her the name Hotlanta and she was gone about eight days before getting put off the show. He sent her home with her clock and she promoted and road that wave as long as she could, she did appearances at clubs but never helped me with any of my rent and did not pay me for watching Kendell, I was pissed. I had to put her out of my house, she was messy and did not help out at all.

I started working at Focus another collection agency and I had to quit quickly because Niecee called CPS and told them that everybody in my house was on drugs. She was angry because Noel stole her laptop. Noel felt like Niecee lived there all that time, trashed the house, we watched her kid and we were owed that. The CPS showed up at my house and drug tested Noel and I. I did not do any drugs so I was not bothered but Noel tested positive for everything. CPS told me if they come back and Noel was there they were going to take my kids. I quit my job because I could not keep her out of my house, I did not trust that she would follow the states rules, I did not even know she snuck a man in my house that was living downstairs, he scared the crap out of me when I saw him walking around my house. Noel had no respect for me while on those drugs, it was time to pack up and go back to Oklahoma. I left Atlanta for good.

Recap— I was in denial, believing I was not going to pay for messing with a married man. I was in denial, believing Noel loved me more than the drugs. I was in denial believing, I knew how to love. I was in denial, believing I could be a good woman to a man. I was in denial, thinking that having sugar daddies did not make me a whore.

CHAPTER SEVEN

LOVE'S RELAPSE

Denial had me believing I was ready for love when I did not even love myself.

It was five years since I saw Denzel and if it were not for my sister I would not have seen him that day.   We had gone to my dad's yearly birthday party in Dallas and Denzel was doing time not too far away. I got over Denzel years ago, we were the best of friends when we talked but my heart was so far gone. I could listen to Denzel and with every conversation praise God that I was over him. My taste in men had grown, I no longer liked thugs, ex gangsters or anything remotely hood. I was into businessmen; every boyfriend I had since Denzel were business owners and very intelligent. We arrived at the prison and my children were so happy to see their dad they cried. I almost did too because I hated that he was not free. He was just as handsome as I remembered. He began to call me frequently after that visit. I knew Denzel loved me but it was all just prison talk for me. You see, Erick and I had recently just broken up so I had nothing else better to do then flirt with my baby daddy.

Erick was a law student; ex-military from Baltimore. I met him working at a club that he owned with some other military guys that were stationed in the city. He was the shy quiet type and that turned me on.

He was a man with a lot of integrity, a workaholic, a man that would be a good role model for my boys. This was right up my alley, had to have him so I started hanging out at his house like a home away from home, it was quiet and my house was always chaotic. Erick had two kids by two different women but they did not live with him. I spent the night whenever I could and he would not even touch me. To be honest, he barely spoke and I did not know if the man liked me or not. One day, I asked does he like sex and he said yes and that he was just respecting me. I thought, I am really needing you to disrespect me right about now but I did not want to come off like a slut.

Erick and I became close although he did not speak much about his feelings or anything for that matter; he was the most guarded man I knew. We had an intimate relationship and I loved him, my kids were spending the night at his house as well and we were real cool. I had fallen in love and could see myself being his wife if I could just get him to open up. I always loved a challenge and this relationship was just that A CHALLENGE. Erick had so much ambition and this bought out the best in me, being around him made me want to better myself. There was not a man alive that had this type of effect on me. I wanted to be the best woman I could possibly be. Leave it to me to let whatever I still felt for Denzel mess it up.

One day Erick found a letter that I had written but never sent off to Denzel and it changed our relationship for the worse. I was never honest about how much I cared about a man to anyone for fear of looking stupid. The letter was talking about my new relationship with Erick and how I liked him but he was ugly. For the life of me I do not know why I used that word because Erick was a real handsome man, nice hair, brown eyes but I took it to the extreme just trying to be funny I guess. Erick said he forgave me but he did not, he started treating me different, he was not available like he used to be anymore. I could tell he was so hurt and I was too because again I let my feelings for Denzel be more important than the man I was dating.

I did everything to get us back on track. I was desperate to have him love me. I went to the tattoo shop to change that Daniel on my breast to Erick. Erick liked the gesture but it was too late. Erick told me he loved me but he did not express it in other ways. I was devastated and the crazy girl from back in the day came out, I started stalking him.

Erick was the reason I went back to school, he nurtured that side of me. He was the reason I went back to church, he was just that type of guy. He moved to a couple of different spots and because I could not come by like I used to I would send emails and blow his phone up, the man would not budge UNTIL.......

Denzel finally got to the half-way house in Oklahoma City May 2010 and things became weird. I took my kids to see him and he was adamant about being with me. I started running into Kara as she was taking her kids there as well. Kara and I had become friends I thought and I really had love for her. We would talk about the kids on the phone from time to time. I would pray for her and she said she would pray for me. I did not want any beef with Kara because I had truly forgiven her for the past. I hoped we could be one big happy family. Kara started treating me funny again. I never understood this because Denzel had always been my boyfriend and then my husband. He had never claimed being Kara's boyfriend even after having kids with her. Clearly Denzel had made her feel like they had a chance when he got out, I did not care one bit if he got with Kara.

The day Denzel got out of the half-way house, he was telling me how much he loved me. He claimed he wanted his family back and would do anything for me to trust him again. The problem with that is the damage was done. Denzel hurt me all the time but I was not built like that, I could never hurt him. He spoke to my family and told them he changed. My mom and sister loved Denzel and told me that God was in this so I needed to give him another chance. It was so hard because I was going against everything I knew. I knew what type of man I wanted, and he did not fit the description. Despite listening to the still soft voice in my head, I went ahead and tried. It was a daily prayer, God if you want me to be with this man help me to gain feelings back for him. Just when I chose to do the right thing, Erick pops up at my job. I had not seen Erick in months and when I saw him I was sick because I loved him and wanted to be with him.

I woke up next to Denzel crying in my sleep, "Baby what's wrong," he said. I kept saying nothing, he was not going for it, "Baby what is the matter," Denzel said frantically, so I told him I had a dream about my granny to pacify him. I was crying because Erick was finally wanting to reconcile and I could not, I had made the choice to be with Denzel. Even though I did not love Denzel like that, I could not go back on my word. I loved Erick but my family made me feel like this is what was best for me and the kids. Denzel went through my phone and saw a text conversation with Erick. The text thread was not bad but he flipped out. I had to remind him, I cut Erick off for him and to give me a minute to adjust because I really had feelings for him.

Denzel got a job working at a car lot and started making decent money, he told me he did not want me to work but just focus on school and he would take care of anything I needed. I knew this to be true because he has always been a provider. I did just that, became a stay at home mom and it worked for us, by this time Jesus had given me everything I prayed for and I fell back in love with Denzel. Denzel was a new man, he was doing everything that I thought a husband should be doing. Denzel was loving, caring, supportive, helping me study, and spending time with me when he was not working. He bought me gifts, bags and shoes, I was really spoiled but that was not new because even in our rough patches he would spoil me. For the first time since the beginning of our relationship my guard was down, I knew he loved me because he showed me.

Kara was not taking our relationship well. I did not expect that she would, but why did I feel guilty for being with my own husband? Denzel called me saying that Kara had a gun sitting on the bed and that she was crying. Denzel had to go over there and talk to her, she went and spent the night in a facility. I flipped out, I cried and reached out to her on Facebook messenger and told her I have felt the same way before, I understand and I love her but she never responded. My heart is different than most even though she was dogging me out, I never returned that type of hatred. Our kids were bonding well but one of them was trouble. Denzel had another child from another woman who he never claimed until he got out of jail. This child must have been raised different because she had no respect, a lot of anger in her and loved to stir up drama. Kara always had her at her house so of course the little girl had it in for me as well, her drama led to a lot of heartache between everybody.

Summer was approaching and I needed to find a way to keep my youngest child busy, he was a pre-teen and already in trouble with the law. He was caught stealing from the neighborhood market and taken to the city jail. I needed help with my boys, Denzel was in the home but not present in my kids life. Denzel worked all day and was only off on Sunday. I knew he honestly meant well but I was expecting more than just financial help when we got back together. I was tired and needed a break. I needed Denzel to be a father and pick up my slack. My boys were trying to run the streets, Raymond would run away every chance he got, he hated I was back with his dad and my oldest who was a daddy's boy since birth was experimenting with drugs. I did not want my baby going down the same road as my other two; I needed a mentor or the big brother program quickly. I ended up enrolling my child into some classes at Todd's Boxing, Todd was military known for mentoring kids and whipping them into shape this sounded like a good fit for us. I eventually started taking a few classes at Todd's as well trying to stay in shape. Everything was going well and if I had any problems with Tommy, I would call his coach.

Denzel rarely took an off day during the week so when he did, I tried to spend that time with him. I decided to skip class one evening and Denzel and I dropped Tommy off for his boxing class. When we came back to pick him up, Todd came to the truck asking how Tommy was doing at home because he had a bad attitude in class and had to pull him to the side and talk to him. Denzel's mannerism instantly changed, he did not like the type of relationship we had and his attitude completely changed. As fine of a man as Denzel was, he was insecure and he always thought I was doing something when I was not, I hated realizing it was because he was the one up to no good. The Coach and I were innocent, we had not done anything remotely disrespectful, yes, the man was fine and I was attracted to him. A fine man was nothing to me I conducted myself like a married woman since Denzel had come back into the picture.

I stopped mentioning anything about boxing to Denzel because at that point he could care less. I made the mistake in confiding in the Coach about Denzel's accusations and that opened the door to him confiding in me about conflicts in his relationship as well. We became very close and talked on the phone multiple times a day about everything. We started working out in the morning before work, he would open the gym and I would meet him at 5:30am. Coach was trying to get back in shape for his job and I was addicted to working out because it helped relieve stress. I liked our relationship. I loved the attention I was getting from Coach. I was not cheating physically but cheating emotionally. Denzel worked so many hours a day, I was lonely for male interaction. I fell into temptation because I was immature and ungodly. I knew better than this, I knew the outcome and did not care enough to do the right thing.

There was a boxing tournament being held in Texas and the Coach invited all the kids to go even if they were not fighting, he also invited me because he needed more chaperones. This is when the affair became sexual, Coach and I went at it like a couple that had not seen each other in months, we had chemistry and the worse part of it all is we became friends so there were feelings involved. Coach still pushed me the same as usual in class and I never let on that anything was going on because that would have crushed my son. We would meet at hotel rooms at least twice a month. We would meet at the movies in the day time on the outskirts of Oklahoma City so we would not be seen. I would clear my phone cache of our calls and text messages everyday which was hard work to remember. But what is done in the dark always comes to the light.

Denzel's probation terms were different than most because he was a sex offender. Sex offenders in Oklahoma were required to provide their address as a part of their probation. The law stated that a sex offender could not live within 2,000 feet of a school, public park or day care facility which made 84 percent of Oklahoma City off-limits to them. Denzel was blessed when he got out of prison to be able to move back to the residence he lived before his conviction because it was a family owned home and the restrictions would not apply to him if he paroled to that same address. Denzel had a few of his clothes there and kept the utilities paid but actually lived with me. After about 18 months of Denzel being out of prison the state changed their rules and even if you owned your home you had to move if close to a school. Denzel was so stressed out he could hardly sleep, he had 30 days to find a home or he would have to move into a motel in which he ended up having to do.

I stopped calling and answering the Coach's calls because Denzel needed me. I could not deal with any distractions and it was just as simple as turning off a light switch. I had never been able to stomach watching Denzel hurt. I put 100 percent into helping him find a home and comforting him. Every night after work Denzel would pick me up to go to the motel we would get there late just to sleep. My mom did me a favor by staying with my kids overnight while we stayed in that filthy motel. Denzel had to have an address to register and since he was at a motel he had to register once a week. The place was the worst, I would not even use the bathroom. I bought our covers from home and burned incense trying to make it smell better but there was not much you could do with soiled carpet. I was Denzel's backbone and no matter what we put each other through I would never turn my back on him or have him stay in that dark place alone. We had to stay overnight at this motel about 3 weeks until Denzel decided to buy one of his older brothers' property's.

The house Denzel decided to buy was 2-story and 4 bedrooms, it was a nice size for the kids but it was in Oklahoma City school district. I was so hurt. I tried my best to find a place in a good school district. I made sure their entire lives to keep them out of inner-city schools. Moving to this house would be failing my kids. I was conflicted, Denzel was proud of the house he was able to provide but no house was worth my kids' education. The school in the district had the worst reputation with the worst test scores in the city. Our relationship was on the verge of ending, I loved the house if it were in a different district. I should've gone with my first mind and kept the house I was renting, if Denzel and I were meant to weather the storms that were forming living in both houses would not matter.

Recap– I was in denial, believing I could be with Denzel without marriage counseling. I was in denial, believing I had forgiven him and could trust him. I was in denial believing Denzel was a changed man. I was in denial, believing he loved me and it was not just prison talk. I was in denial, believing our families could blend with no hard feelings. I was in denial, believing Kara was my friend.

CHAPTER EIGHT

TEAR DROPS

Denial had me believing my cheating was justifiable.

I cried real tears moving out of the rent house. Tommy began going to the inner-city school and I was depressed. I saw a change in Denzel's attitude, I thought initially it was because I was unhappy. I soon found out by going through his phone that there was another woman. I called the number back from his phone that was calling to hear an Alicia Keys ringtone of the same song that he said reminded him of me. I instantly lost my mind. Why did not I keep my rent house? I could have kept my kids in their school. Now I am stuck in the same relationship I left 10 years ago.

We fought, we screamed, we said the most hurtful things to each other, his words cut deep and in retaliation I cut back. I hated our relationship, even when I did everything in my power to get back on track, we never could. Days turned into weeks of us just existing in two different worlds. We were still sexually active being the only part of our relationship that was intimate. Just when things started getting better and we were talking again like partners, Denzel went through my phone. He read a text from Coach saying he missed me and everything we used to do. I could not believe I got caught slipping like that. I had not talked to the Coach in about a year and had not even responded to the text. Denzel set up counseling sessions and we went once a week trying to get to the bottom of our issues. I tried being proactive by being honest about the relationship wanting him to understand why I had the affair. Denzel never confided in me in return to tell me his why, who or when so I did not trust we were getting anywhere. We continued counseling for about two months and never went back. We needed Jesus and years of counseling, this was not your typical relationship. We had a date night at least three times a month and he bought me anything I wanted so I just rolled with it. We tried taking a few trips and we had fun. It was not all bad and we had our good days. We just did not trust each other. I loved our relationship minus our cheating and kids.

We did not agree when it came to our kids, I wanted him to be a disciplinarian, he felt like he was gone too long and did not feel comfortable. We were raised different and had different views on religion and relationships. I believed without Jesus we had nothing and with Jesus we had everything. He woke up to rap music, I woke up to the Christian television station. I wanted him to cut back on his hours at work so we could have family time and could pay more attention to the kids but he had other dreams.

Denzel's kids hated my kids and it did not help our relationship. They hated that I was with their dad and that my kids and their dad were under the same roof. Every time they came over it ended in Denzel and I arguing and his kids stealing from my kids. Denzel would not say a word, he already felt guilty for not being there while they were growing up. He enabled their actions. I felt he did nothing to protect us, he did not care at all that his kids were disrespectful to me or to the kids. My baby boy wanted to be accepted so bad that it took him years to confess everything that they were doing to him. My daughter was the same way just wanting to fit in with them.

Denzel continued to work from 8am–10pm 6 days a week and I was lonely for male attention like desperate housewives only I was working 2 jobs and in school. When my ex-boyfriend Erick called and asked if I would bartend at his new club opening, I obliged quickly after he said he would pay $100.00 a night plus tips. Initially we were just co-workers but that changed as soon as I felt Denzel getting distant. That was just an excuse for me to do what I wanted to do. Denzel said things like I do not care about nothing I cannot control to send me overboard, his pimp mentality was getting the best of me.

Denzel could not control me and that was the problem. I told myself I was never going to cheat again after the Coach but why not he did not believe me anyway.

Working with Erick brought back mixed emotions, I wanted him physically but emotionally, that boat sailed. My emotions were wrapped up in Denzel. Erick did not trust me, so he was nonchalant when I spoke of working it out. Most nights I worked with Erick I felt bad because I knew I was being deceitful. Denzel would hate me if he found out I was working for my ex. I would not tell Erick anything about Denzel. But I made the mistake one time of telling him one of Denzel's slick comments and he laughed so hard I was embarrassed. Erick said I told you that dude had not changed but you did not believe me.

It was not until I ran my second marathon that I decided to cheat. The first marathon I ran Denzel was supportive, it meant the world to me. The second one he did not show up just like he was not showing up in the relationship. I was devastated he was not invested in me anymore but Erick was there for me more than ever. Every night we closed the club down we were intimate. Then one night getting home from work Denzel rolled over wanting to have sex. I had sex with Erick not even an hour ago, I did not know what to do. I have never turned down sex, he would know I was cheating so I went with it, while we had sex tears streamed down my face and I told myself I would cut it off with Erick, I did not. We continued to have sex until the club shut down. It stayed open from April thru July. The club never jumped off because of the location, nobody including myself wanted to drive to that area of town. Erick moved to North Carolina shortly after and told me I could come with him. I just knew there was no way to run from the situation I created plus I wanted to finish school.

Denzel gave me anything I wanted. I was in denial believing it was love. I was addicted to shopping and he fed my addiction, it was a love replacement. Every time he made me angry or I felt lonely I shopped. I had as many sneakers as I had heels, I had as many heels as I had boots. I believed that his daughter was destroying my stuff.

She was in the middle of all our problems. Nameless' mother was in and out of jail so nameless was from house to house, I asked Denzel to let her come live with us and all hell broke loose. She was the devil in my life. My children used to argue but now they fight, she would listen to my conversations and start mess between Kara and me. It was like a hurricane came through my house, any peace that we had was destroyed. She was like an STD that you could not cure. She would bring up the fights Kara and I had to get the other kids upset. She was miserable and jealous hearted but who could blame her, it was like she was raised by wolves. I tried looking out for her, if I loved Denzel, I have to love her, right? She did not appreciate anything, the more my daughter gave to her the more she stole, I wanted to kill her.

Christmas Eve and I am running around the stores trying to make my money split 7 ways, Denzel was not in good shape financially so I told him I would take care of his girls and my four. Christmas day came and he only bought for Kara's kids and nameless after I could not buy my kids what I wanted to buy them, that was it for me. I was no longer doing it. I needed a break and I could not stomach the disrespect. My sister's best friend Lomita told me that God has cleared you to leave that Denzel's heart had left me and I was devastated. I cried to my daughter she had just come back home from living with ManMan's girlfriend for a while after we had gotten into it, like I said before, nameless had us all at war.

New Year's was the first night Denzel did not come home. He told me he was going out of town with his boys, I knew he was lying. He was going to spend the night with the same woman that was stalking my fakebook page. In November, I made a post that said men are always with their families on holidays and like any woman she was in his ear hard about spending a holiday with her. I was sick the entire night and could only imagine what they were doing. He got home around 6pm the next day, I wanted to kill him because now he was being blatantly disrespectful. I bought a ticket to Detroit to see my best friend Ginger, I needed her and I needed to get away while. I was there my kids called me to tell me that Kara's kids came and stole their clothes, bleached the one present my youngest son got for Christmas, and stole his PlayStation. Nameless took all my daughters Jordan's and clothes she bought, I was sick and in Detroit snowed in. Denzel did not do anything, he did not even try to get my kids' belongings back, I thought I was going to die.

Mentally I was stuck, I leaned on God. The best part of me was God, he was and will always be my go too. I had no excuses for putting myself back in the predicament I was in. Denzel did not love me and he had never loved me because love doesn't hurt. I blocked out what he was doing started confiding in my homeboy Claude. I knew Claude from back in the day when he was a high school basketball star, his stats were off the chain. He was an ear, nothing sexual and nothing potentially sexual he was just a great friend. Banana Girl had a cheerleading competition in Dallas, so I asked him to roll with me, which was another quick get a way that was needed. Denzel never paid attention to me but he paid attention to me that weekend, his suspicions were way off, he had a car wreck that weekend as well so instead of enjoying myself like I should've been I was worried about him. He questioned about who I was with and of course I lied because he would have thought it was more than just two friends going out of town to support Marcia and Banana Girl, he and Marcia were tight as well so I took it as if it were a family trip.

The Memorial Marathon came and went again and of course like every year, I ached and pained but this year was different. This was the second year I cried because Denzel and I were even worse off than the year before. I caught strep throat and was extremely sick the following Monday and was sent home from work, that was the third night he did not come home. I was pissed, I could not even move while he was out doing Lord knows what with Lord knows who. He started hanging out with a twenty something year old boy around my oldest son's age, I thought he was going through a mid-life crisis. Why would not I just leave? I would not leave because I wanted him to pay for ruining my life. When he got out of prison, he was placed on probation for three years, for three years he could not drink or smoke so for three years I did not drink trying to be supportive. As soon as he got off probation it was like de'Jawn who.

Denzel came home one evening distraught, if he was a white man, he would have been pale. He was despondent like he had seen a ghost. I thought one of my children were hurt or was killed, he said he had to talk to me and told me he got a girl pregnant. I thought I was going to lose my mind. This was a different sick. I could not eat, sleep or work. Denzel knew me and knew I would kill that girl if I found out who she was, so he kept her a secret. For the life of me I could not figure out who this woman was, it turned out she was not a woman she was a little girl. This grown man got a girl his daughter's age pregnant. What would I look like talking to her, I wanted to talk to her mother. I was not anything like Denzel and did not associate with kids like they adults. What does he even talk about with a girl that age, I had to process. I always thought Denzel was immature and his thought process was off, he hung out with his daughter's friends at her college. His mentality was that of a twenty something year old and a grown woman besides me would not want any part of that. I was just suckered in because I was already married to him and thought it would be nice to have their dad in the home.

I had a great relationship with my boss at work, they loved and understood the attack I was under and gave me as much time as I needed off work. My bosses were Christian, every morning they prayed that I could find strength. When I came home from work, I would get right in the bed. I put trash bags over my windows because I wanted it completely dark. I was in a dark place, I wanted to sleep and never wake up but I loved my kids way too much to put them through that. It was like I was already dead, my youngest son had to fend for himself. I was sick, I had just enough strength to make it to work for five or six hours, when I walked in the house I went right up the stairs to my room and shut the door. I had not even seen my kitchen in weeks. Tommy started acting out, he felt like he lost both parents because Denzel moved in with his Uncle.

My mom enrolled me in a ministry class so I could get grief counseling, it helped most days. However, I did not hear anything they were saying, it was like I was just existing. I had little strength, most days I did not remember even drinking water much less eating food. I kept every television in the house on TBN, I never turned the station, I could not stomach watching regular TV. My beautiful daughter was pregnant too. It was like I could not even be happy for her because the thought of Denzel having another baby was rotting my insides. How could something as beautiful as a woman being pregnant cause so much pain. He used to lie about getting Kara pregnant or say I do not know who she's pregnant by, he used to spare my feelings or just would not even tell me. The last two kids Kara had I did not even know about until they were born. This time felt different. He told me he took her to get an abortion, but she changed her mind when they got there. He said he did not want to have any more kids and that he was just as hurt as me.

This was a bad dream that I could not wake up from, why did I still want him? I did not, I just wanted to win like he was a prize. I knew I could do better than Denzel, I knew I was miserable with him and until I let him go completely, I would never find true happiness. I did not have the passion or the energy to chase Denzel anymore. I was chasing God. I needed a touch from the Lord. I knew he was there and I needed to feel his presence. God protected me, Denzel and the girl because if I had found out who she was at that time, she would not have been carrying his baby and I would have been in jail over a man that did not even love me.

My birthday was near, and I needed my friend. The only woman in this world that could get me out of this funk was Ginger. She flew down and it worked, I was not embarrassed about how I let the house go, by this time I had not even seen my living room, den or kitchen in over six weeks. When Ginger got to my house, she made me take the trash bags off the window. Denzel paid for me to have a few parties, even though he was not in the house he still came over to bring me money and see Ginger. The night of my last birthday party he did not show up like promised. I was on the phone with a suicidal hotline getting prayer all night. This is the first year he missed my parties. I always had at least three parties the week of my birthday. Before Ginger left to go back to Detroit, she was adamant about me cleaning the entire house and garage. It made me feel eighty percent better, I cried like a baby when my friend left.

Denzel and I were talking a lot more than during the summertime, I was working on myself and reading the bible and self-help books. I was able to take better care of my daughter while she was going through her pregnancy because I was able to start processing what was going on in my life. For my daughter's birthday she wanted to have a family dinner, her dad showed up we started talking again heavy and he moved back home. I knew he was coming home soon because he started entertaining longer conversations and started meeting me at church on Wednesdays and Sundays.

Now that he was back home it felt like a honeymoon stage, we made love every day. We did not speak about him having a baby we just focused on us. Our relationship felt stronger than it had been in the last two years. He started going to the studio with me again, music was my outlet, he was always supportive, and I trusted his ear. I knew it was only a matter of time for the relationship to get ugly again but for the time being I was riding the wave. To be honest, it felt like a happy home as long as I stayed in denial about their being a baby on the way. I did not know what was going on between him and the girl and did not care, he was meeting my superficial needs. I did know that this was the last year I was going to be with Denzel. I did not know exactly when I was leaving but I would change my life before I turned forty. I would not be in that house celebrating my next birthday. Reality was that after he had the baby it was over for us.

I told Denzel it was our last Christmas together and bought him everything I could think that he wanted. He always bought me the best gifts, we had a good quiet Christmas he knew his kids could not come back to our house while I was there. New Year's Eve I went to a church service and Denzel stayed home, I asked God to please give me the strength to leave Denzel for good and leaving church I knew God would answer my prayers.

Denzel had his baby the first week in January and to my surprise he
was very respectful about it. He came home right afterwards, and I
was supportive because I knew in my heart I was leaving him soon.
He finally told me after the baby was born that it was a girl that
worked with him. Made since the reason he kept it a secret because
he knows I would have been up at his job wrecking shop. After his
child was born, I was more submissive than I had ever been because I
wanted to keep him home, I set a sexy mood every night and he loved
it. He never brought up his other kids, I think he was trying to spare
my feelings but that was keeping me in denial. Denzel became distant
again, I was used to it and kept my plans with moving. Our seven-
teen-year wedding anniversary was in April, we did our normal but I
was saving my pennies and planning my escape.

Recap– I was in denial, believing that God wanted my
marriage saved. I was in denial, believing I could let Denzel lead me without him letting God lead him. I was in
denial, believing I could dumb myself down and go against
all I believed and submit to Denzel. I was in denial, believing I could handle another year with Denzel. I was in
denial, believing I could love, trust and respect Denzel.

CHAPTER NINE

ESCAPE

I was in denial believing my healing was complete when I escaped.

My escape was not physical it was mental. I could not escape physically until I escaped mentally but I still needed time to heal. I had to change my mind, if I did not change my mind about my life then I could not change my heart. If my emotions told me to call that dude and cuss him out then that is what I did. If my emotions told me to call another man then that is what I did its crazy how when your relationship is going good you are able to entertain other men's conversation but when you are losing the man you love, you only want him. I did not know how to take my feelings out of my situation and look from the outside in. I just kept making excuses for him because I was not ready to go through the separation anxiety. I did not want to feel like I was just giving the little young trick my husband. I knew Jesus could do anything; he could save my marriage and open Denzel's eyes to see what his cheating was doing to our marriage. At this point it was not his cheating because I was used to that, it was the boldness, his honesty about this being his baby and how she was good girl. Denzel had never talked good about any girl to me he would always down play them. I knew he could not possibly love me doing me like this. My thinking was corrupt; I had gotten so used to this kind of treatment, I thought I was a slave to Denzel, but I was a slave to my mind.

Denzel learned to manipulate over the years. That is what pimps do, they find creative ways to manipulate women, and he actually told me everything was going to be his way or it was not going to work. He had never spoken to me this way, I do not know how he treated other women but he kept me on a pedestal. I had grown up too much and his words meant nothing anymore, he was not even making sense. I soon realized that was because he did not respect or love me, he just said whatever hurtful thing that came to mind. I battled with trying to figure out the root of his issues and not even realizing mine. Denzel was not the problem, I was the problem. Our values were different, I could never smoke weed with my kids, I could hang with my kids in a respectful way. Denzel's dad and uncle glorified pimping, his dad was his best friend. Denzel must think he is pleasing his dad because now again he is talking about how many different women he has doing different things for him. I was coming up on my 40th birthday and I promised myself that was the cut-off age. I was no longer living my life unhappy. I like to travel, we only had one more child under 18 at home. I could not wait for the day that I did not have to hide snacks, fuss over my leftovers being eaten, deal with everybody's attitudes and walk around the house naked if I wanted to.

It was time to make my move. I had prepared mentally and financially by staying prayed up and saving money. I bought a brand new bedroom suite a couple months before and stored it in my sister's garage. I had taken the necessary steps to get out of the house of pain. I brought boxes from work and had everything organized but Denzel did not think I would leave because I had packed up and threatened leaving for over a year. I had lived out of those boxes for a while. We tried to work it out over and over again but every conversation just ended up with an argument. It was just too much hurt there. Denzel was not a man of God and I am all about God. We never stopped having sex, that part we were good at but I made up in my mind when I left that house I would never have sex with him again.

 Chris picked me up and we went looking for apartments on the fourth of July. The first apartments I went to were Ashford Park, I always thought these apartments were classy looking, gated community, a small complex, and very quiet. The manager took us to look at the apartment available and I loved it, I filled out the application and paid the application fee. I figured I would stop looking and wait to hear from Ashford Park since my heart was set on them, my sister dropped me off and before she even got home they called me and told me I was approved. I could not believe how fast God moved, it was a holiday everything was closed so they never did the background check or checked my references this was one of the many miracles that God performed for me. I did not even have to pay the deposit. All I had to pay was the prorated half month rent when I moved in on the 15th. The special was first month rent and second month half off. WONT HE DO IT?

I hired movers. I had my furniture delivered. I had a handy man put my bedroom suite together, paid deposits on utilities, put in a change of address at the post office and changed my address on my license. I was so ready to move and my birthday was in a month so I was right on track to be moved out before I turned 40. I took off work the day of my move so I had all day to get my new home just the way I liked it. I actually told Denzel I was moving the day before I left and asked him to come home early to chill with me, he did not believe me. I do not know why I wanted to spend time with him at this monumental time in my life.

The first night at my new home was mentally hard. I wrestled between just going back to my old house or toughing it out. I asked my handyman who Denzel adopted into the family and called him his uncle to spend the night. He agreed to stay so I could get through the night while reassuring me that I can make it and that I was doing the right thing. I knew if I could get through the first night I would never go back and I did not.

Life was starting to look up, I had my new place, eating better, feeling better and looking better. Denzel and I still talked on the phone every day, he had the nerve to be mad that I left like I did him wrong. I came over a couple of times in the morning doing things for my son and we would argue because we still were emotional. I left and that was my first step, I was proud to be getting my life on track. I still wanted to know he cared, I called him to say that I was hungry periodically just to hear his response. I wanted to hear him say come get some money that would make me feel like I was still his responsibility. When he stopped paying my car note I knew he did not care about my wellbeing anymore.

My birthday was approaching, Denzel said he wanted to take me to the movies if he got off early, to me that meant he was not concerned. It did not hurt my feelings one bit that he did not come thru on his word because I never believed he would anyway. I went to Atlanta the following day to visit Ginger and Nakia, we had a ball. I went to church with Nakia and while clapping my hands my wedding ring broke. I knew God was telling me to totally dead the situation in my mind about Denzel.

Herman a man that was in my messenger hit me up asking if I was back in town, he knew I had been out of town because he messaged me on my birthday to see what was up. I thought he was fine, I did not know much about him, only that he had a band that played in a lot of the night clubs around town. Every time we saw each other we hugged in passing, I admired him because after his band finished playing he never stuck around, I thought whoever he was going home to was a lucky lady. Ginger flew back home with me to stay a couple of weeks because in my mind my birthday was the entire month.

Herman in boxed me on messenger asking for my number and to take me out, I obliged but let him know I had my best friend in town and my sister from another mister Chametra with me. He was cool with that and came to pick us up and took us to his friend's wife's birthday party. We had a great time, we drank, we danced, and we laughed. He dropped us off and came back about the next day to take us to lunch. When we got back to my house, I told him I felt like he was going to be my husband, we laughed but I was serious.

I wrote a list of what I wanted in a man and I would not settle for anything less. I made my mind up to be the best woman possible. I read books about marriage and relationship before Denzel moved back in thinking I was preparing for him but I was actually preparing for my next relationship. Reading about men helped me understand how much women were different and how their minds worked. I did not want to hurt another man and was tired of hurting myself. The man I chose had to have a personal relationship with God, not just go to church but I needed to feel the presence of the Lord in their life. I was not getting into a relationship if I felt the man was not led by God or if I felt I had to be completely guarded, I wanted to be open and free. I did not want any secrets, I wanted him to know the good the bad and the ugly. My preacher said women who picked the wrong type of men had a broken picker, my picker was fixed. Whoever I got in a relationship with I would be proud to be on his arm and I would give the upmost respect from the beginning.

Herman was a dream come true; he was everything I thought I ever wanted. He was chocolate, beautiful complexion, nice smile, muscular build and ten years older than me. He was a carpenter and owned his own business, he could literally build a house. I was attracted to men that worked with their hands that knew how to fix everything that meant never having to call a handyman. This man was a mechanic as well. I did not expect to get with a man a month after leaving my husband. I knew I wanted a man of God and it turned out Herman was the Minister of Music at his church. We had so much in common, I loved watching bands, both of our dads were preachers, we both grew up in church, both created music, we drank the same liquor, neither of us did any drugs, we both love Dallas Cowboys, we both love Sci-Fi movies, we just fit. I saw Herman every day since the first date and within one month we were saying I love you. I loved the way he treated me, he was so gentle, kind and understanding.

I had no time to be single, I was with Herman too soon and that was not healthy. I found out that just because I was with Herman, I was not over Denzel. Ginger came from home from Dollar General, she said she thought she saw Denzel in the car with another woman and he turned down the street before my apartments. I grabbed the keys and ran out with a vengeance ready to fight, I did not see him on the next block. That evening I asked Herman to make love to me and told him I did not want to love Denzel anymore; he was all for that and we had sex. There was a saying, to get over one man get up under another man; that was a worldly saying not a Godly saying. We were only together for three weeks but since the first night we met, he spent the night every night. Having sex with him worked, I transferred emotions which was a terrible mistake because I made a promise to stay celibate until marriage.

The first year with Herman was the best year I have ever had in my life. I felt like I was finally grown, I had no kids in the house and I did whatever I wanted to do. We took five trips in one year from the east coast to the west coast. He took me on my first cruise for my birthday and one-year anniversary. We never had one fight, Herman was not the type to argue, he knew how to talk to me and checked me a few times about communicating and learning how to address issues properly. I think God sent my soulmate.

My man check list that I prayed about was missing something. I did not know it was missing until I found out we had a problem. Herman loved the casino but that was not the problem. The problem was when he went, he did not answer the phone and he spent hours. He could sit in the casino for eight hours easy. Not only was I getting out of a relationship with infidelity issues but I had catastrophic thinking. When I did not hear from him, I thought he was in a ditch somewhere or in the hospital. This started to get ugly, I told him just tell me when he was going to the casino so I would not worry. I think he felt like he was checking in and he did not like it or maybe it was the thrill of feeling like he was sneaking off. It did not matter how much I told him I did not care about him going to the casino he still called himself sneaking off. He told me I knew where he was just come up there but

I shouldn't have to do that although a few times I did and there he was.

I loved Herman and I was not going to make the mistake of not getting a divorce like I did when Daniel wanted to marry me. I decided to file for divorce when Tommy turned eighteen because in the state of Oklahoma you would have to go through counseling if you had minor kids. Tommy's birthday passed and I needed the push and got it from my daughter who called crying over her dad. Missy never cried so when she did I took it to heart, she felt like her dad did not care about her because he put her out of his house. It was only two months after Tommy's birthday, I filed one month shy of Herman and I second anniversary of being together. When my divorce was finalized I felt like the happiest woman in the world, I overcame.

Recap— I was in denial, I believing I loved myself because I finally left. I was in denial, believing Herman's love would help with my healing.

CHAPTER TEN

MARVELOUS

I was in denial, believing my motives were genuine for marriage.

I wanted to get married after getting a divorce, the court said I would have to wait six months by law. Herman and I had a wonderful relationship, we still had not had one fight, he was not an argumentative man and he never raised his voice. Herman's demeanor and outlook on life was the balance I needed. His laid-back personality wore off on me in a good way, so where was my ring? The first year of our relationship we talked about marriage all the time. I thought we were on the same page.

We were going on our second annual cruise and I knew he was going to propose. Not only did his family look at us a certain way for not being married but I was ready. The conviction was strong because having sex without being married was wrong. We did not live together but we spent the night with each other every night, I could not understand what the holdup was but needless to say we had our first fight on the cruise. Patrice went on the cruise with us and I told her I tore our cabin up looking for my ring and could not find it, she laughed but I did not think it was funny. My attitude was horrible I was breaking up with Herman because I felt he was leading me on, I knew he liked me a lot but now I was struggling with the idea of it not being love. The week we got home from the cruise he bought me a Mercedes-Benz; it was so beautiful that I forgot all about the ring for a couple of months.

Every time I wanted to break up with Herman it was because he would not make music with me or he had not proposed. Each holiday that passed was the perfect opportunity in my eyes, that was not being taken. I am a writer and Herman is a composer there was no reason in the world that we were not writing our own worship songs for the church worship team, he was always too busy to make music and writing music is what I was born to do. I wrestled with my decision because those were our only problems besides his casino addiction that would eventually be a problem if we lacked in finances down the road.

Fast-forward to our fourth annual cruise, I did not care anymore. I did not care about looking good. I did not bring dresses for the formal nights. I did not bring a bathing suit, I was tired of caring. I did not care if he spent all his time in the casino on the boat. At home, I did not care if he took me out, I stopped caring if he went to the casino and stayed all night without calling. I was tired of putting forth an effort for a man that did not see himself being my husband. He was still my best friend and we still had fun, I just had no expectation. I still went to his house every day after work but it was not important that we watched football together, ate together, he could sleep on the couch all night and it would not bother me. I recognized my patterns. I was in and out of love, one minute I felt like I wanted to be married, the next minute I wanted to be single. I was following his patterns. Herman was never mean and almost always in a good mood but I could feel the difference when he was in love and when he just loved me. It could be a movie that changed my mind or a church sermon.

It seemed like every six months Herman would bring up the fact that he wanted to marry me and I would get excited. But then that thought disappeared from his mind. I kept trying to back away from him, but I had no reason, he was a great boyfriend. Herman was affectionate and took great care of me. I could not figure out why he did not want me as his wife. Herman's first marriage took a toll on him. He said it was the worst time of his life and he did not know the woman he married and she changed after they said I do. He felt the pressure from his mom to marry her because they were living together. I kept trying to reassure him that I was not her and I would not change on him, what he sees is what he gets.

I started to re-evaluate myself and question my motives, why did I want to get married? Yes, I wanted to please God, but was I even ready for marriage? I am a selfish person and stuck in my ways. I realized two things; one, I wanted Denzel to know I could move on quickly with my life and two, another man would want to marry me. Did I want to marry Herman more than I wanted Denzel to know I could move on with my life? Denzel was still inadvertently controlling me. It changed me instantly, I stopped looking for a ring from

Herman. My struggle is abstaining from sex. Herman told me our plans were to get married, so I have been in denial all these years thinking it was okay but knowing it is not. I pray for strength every day for celibacy.

I am a loyal person at heart, it would not be cheating if I dated other people because I am not married. I am dating a man that is comfortable not marrying me. I have to make a decision if I can continue dating someone that does not take my feelings in consideration about marriage. I have to trust God more and let him lead. Just because I believe I have a great relationship does not mean God does not have something greater for me. His ways are not our ways. With our relationship as good as I believe it is, I do not have the urge to date but being with Herman makes me feel like I am not good enough for a ring or worthy to be someone's wife. Everybody is not meant to get married, a hard pill to swallow when you want a mate.

TO BE CONTINUED

ABOUT THE AUTHOR

Author de'Jawn is a writer of all genres of music, she is not limited to rap and rhythm and blues, all she needs is the beat and a little bit of time. She appreciates country, rock and roll, jazz, and poetry. Music is not her passion, it is her addiction, she will say "there is nothing that gets me higher, it motivates me, relaxes me, soothes me, stabilizes my mind, music is universal " in her own words. As a songwriter and now author, she desires her audience to feel every emotion that she is feeling while creating, my happiness, awkwardness, sarcasm, confidence, pain and laughter but most importantly my authenticity in her words. In a world full of hate she wants to show love the best way she knows how, with hopes to make that lonely person feel like they're not alone in their thoughts. If she can get people to forget their problems for a moment by listening to the music her team creates, she'll feel accomplished, she doesn't want to make music that hurts or influences wrongful acts, she was put on the earth to show love!

www.ingramcontent.com/pod-product-compliance
Lightning Source LLC
Chambersburg PA
CBHW051932240626
47153CB00004B/1462